STRANGE HARBORS

STRANGE HARBORS

Edited by John Biguenet
and Sidney Wade

TWO LINES   WORLD WRITING IN TRANSLATION   XV

FOUNDING EDITOR   *Olivia E. Sears*

POETRY EDITOR   *Sidney Wade*

PROSE EDITOR   *John Biguenet*

PUBLICATIONS MANAGER   *Annie Janusch*

Endpaper: Nuala Ní Dhomhnaill, "Ceist na Teangan" from *Pharaoh's Daughter* (Wake Forest University Press, 1993), translated by Ivy Porpotage.

Strange Harbors
TWO LINES World Writing in Translation
no. 15

Cover photos by Kristen Gleason and Tag Savage
Text composition by Tag Savage, based on an original design by Rudy Garibay

Printed in Canada by Friesens Corporation

Distributed by The University of Washington Press

TWO LINES is indexed in the MLA International Bibliography.

For Gregory and Clementine Rabassa, who have piloted

a lifetime of translations to safe harbor in English.

Contents

Editors' Notes

To celebrate our 15th anniversary, we invited two renowned writers and translators, Pulitzer-nominated playwright and novelist John Biguenet and poet and Turkish translator Sidney Wade, to guest edit the 2008 edition of TWO LINES World Writing in Translation. The two bring very different perspectives, and their collaboration results in a fascinating collage of international literature. This vibrant anthology includes poetry by distinguished writers that is so fresh it has yet to appear in print even in the original (like Emmanuel Moses translated by Marilyn Hacker), previews from forthcoming novels in translation by some of the world's greatest writers and translators (like

Antonio Muñoz Molina translated by Edith Grossman), and our first special section with a regional focus, this year a tour of contemporary Turkish poetry. Enjoy your journey!

OLIVIA E. SEARS, FOUNDING EDITOR

We tell ourselves it's universal, storytelling. It is—except what it is a storyteller tells isn't always and everywhere the same thing. Reading stories in translation, one soon begins to wonder, "What is a story?"

One might as well ask, "What is love?" We think it universal. We think we know what others mean when they use the word. But reading translated stories about love, who can keep from asking, "Can this be love, the thing the story—if it is a story—talks about?"

We concede we do not always understand ideas. What makes us think we understand emotions any better?

So we take ship in a vessel refitted in English to some strange harbor, where we might learn, at last, the answers to such questions. We never do, of course. And we journey on to the next harbor and the next, grateful to the shipwrights who have made our hopeless voyage possible.

JOHN BIGUENET

Strange Harbors, indeed! I'm delighted with my coeditor John Biguenet's discovery of this theme in the submissions. My experience of reading through each and every poem in this volume, as well as so many that could not be accommodated because of space constraints, was like sailing into many strange new ports of call—acquainting myself visually and then viscerally with the unfamiliar but fetching and passing strange new forms, outlines, smells, sounds, and colors. Good mystery resonates throughout each of these poems—questions that will never be answered but whose explanations are not, finally, necessary, because the substance of each poem in

English is so well-crafted and profoundly alluring. Of course most of us will never really hear or understand the full spectrum of these poems' conversations with the literature of their homelands, unless we are perfectly bilingual ourselves and completely familiar with the development of their cultures, but we are compensated for that lack by the fragrance and texture of the new skins in which these translations live in English. The width and depth of experience here is also a great gift—these are poems that could never have been written first in English, as their necessities so clearly reside in the soil and local waters of their native cultures. I was struck by the ubiquity of water here, in the form of rain, rivers, shores, and I felt it a great privilege to travel these roads and waterways, and I hope you derive as much pleasure from these many voices from the far corners and harbors of the world. They're brave and new and full of surprises, and never, finally, foreign.

SIDNEY WADE

STRANGE HARBORS

Two Poems by Jibanananda Das

Translated by Jordan Mills Pleasant and Devadatta Joardar from Bengali (East Bengal, now Bangladesh)

These two poems are taken from my current project, with Devadatta Joardar, of translating a comprehensive selection of the poems of Jibanananda Das from Bengali into English. This project would have been impossible without the generous support of the Friends of India Endowment of Athens, Ohio, and the Ohio University Honors Tutorial College.

Jibanananda Das was born in Barisol in modern Bangladesh in 1899, lived in Kolkata during the 1947 Partition of India, and died there in 1954, having been bisected by a tram. He is probably the most famous Bengali poet, second to the Nobel Prize-winning Rabindranath Tagore, and is generally considered both a depressive romantic and a nature poet. His most famous collection might be *Ruposhi Bangla* (*Bengal the Beautiful*) in which he revolutionized both the sonnet and the Bengali language with an alarming return to epic Sanskrit prosody. Das' talent for juxtaposing tragic opposites is often startling. Dreamy and surreal, his poetry is charged with nature and man, life and death.

"If I Became" illustrates each of these qualities most poignantly. Readers are faced with a peaceful ideal of the natural world through the first-person experience of a duck's romance, which ideal is violently shattered by the foreign explosion of a hunter's deadly shot. "The Two Small Black Hands of the Clock," on the other hand, reveals how Das' simple and eloquent language can elucidate certain aspects of the human condition so accurately. Although each of these translations tries to replicate the original Bengali meter, neither illustrates Das' mastery of formal verse. Both, however, demonstrate Das' mastery of experimental verse.

The translation process has been arduous but gratifying. I have often translated formal poetry, and although much of the poetry of Jibanananda Das is informal, it is informal only insofar as the priest poets of our own tradition are informal—the novelty of form and prosody coupled with the content of a given poem fuses the whole into a formal, albeit unconventional, masterpiece. I am elated to have had the opportunity to translate these poems from Bengali, and I am even more elated that English-reading audiences will finally have the opportunity to experience this most intriguing verse of the Bengali language.

JORDAN MILLS PLEASANT

Original text: Jibanananda Das, "Àmi jadi hatàm," first published in *Banalatà Sen*. Kolkata: Kavità Bhavan, 1942. "Ghorir duiti choto hàt dhire," first published in *Jibanananda Dàser kàvyasamagra*. Kolkata: Bhàravi, 2001.

ঘড়ির দুইটি ছোটো কালো হাত ধীরে

ঘড়ির দুইটি ছোটো কালো হাত ধীরে
আমাদের দু-জনকে নিতে চায় যেই শব্দহীন মাটি ঘাসে
সাহস সংকল্প প্রেম আমাদের কোনোদিন সেদিকে যাবে না
তবুও পায়ের চিহ্ন সেদিকেই চলে যায় কী গভীর সহজ অভ্যাসে।

কবিতা। পৌষ ১৩৬১

The Two Small Black Hands of the Clock

The two small black hands of the clock want to take
the two of us slowly to that silent earth and its grass,
but our courage, resolve, and love will never go that way—
yet our footprints move there, driven by some deep, simple habit.

আমি যদি হতাম

আমি যদি হতাম বনহংস,
বনহংসী হতে যদি তুমি,
কোনো এক দিগন্তের জলসিড়ি নদীর ধারে
ধানক্ষেতের কাছে
ছিপছিপে শরের ভিতর
এক নিরালা নীড়ে ;

তা হলে আজ এই ফাল্গুনের রাতে
ঝাউয়ের শাখার পেছনে চাঁদ উঠতে দেখে
আমরা নিম্নভূমির জলের গন্ধ ছেড়ে
আকাশের রুপালি শস্যের ভিতর গা ভাসিয়ে দিতাম—
তোমার পাখনায় আমার পালক, আমার পাখায় তোমার রক্তের স্পন্দন—
নীল আকাশে খইক্ষেতের সোনালি ফুলের মতো অজস্র তারা,
শিরীষ বনের সবুজ রোমশ নীড়ে
সোনার ডিমের মতো
ফাল্গুনের চাঁদ ।

If I Became

If I became a woodland gander
and you became a woodland goose,
then we would make our lonely nest
among some slender reeds
beside a paddy field,
down a little distance where the Jalsiri river flows.

We would watch the moon
rise behind the branches of tamarisk trees on autumn nights
then, leaving the scent of the lowland waters behind,
we would drift into the sky's silver harvest—
my feathers in your wings, in my wings the stirring of your blood—
the stars up in the sky would be as countless golden flowers in the fields,
and our cozy nest would be made of wild raintree flowers.
And like a golden egg,
the autumn moon.

হয়তো গুলির শব্দ :
আমাদের তির্যক গতিস্রোত,
আমাদের পাখায় পিস্টনের উল্লাস,
আমাদের কণ্ঠে উত্তর হাওয়ার গান !
হয়তো গুলির শব্দ আবার :
আমাদের স্তব্ধতা,
আমাদের শান্তি ।
আজকের জীবনের এই টুকরো টুকরো মৃত্যু আর থাকত না,
থাকত না আজকের জীবনের টুকরো টুকরো সাধের ব্যর্থতা ও অন্ধকার ;
আমি যদি বনহংস হতাম,
বনহংসী হতে যদি তুমি ;
কোনো এক দিগন্তের জলসিঁড়ি নদীর ধারে
ধানক্ষেতের কাছে ।

Perhaps then, a bullet would ring out
on our wavering course,
our wings fluttering with a piston's ecstasy
and the song of the north resounding from our throats!
Perhaps then, a bullet would ring out:
our silence,
our peace.
Death's fragments would be no more in our lives;
no more, the fragments of unfulfilled longing and darkness in our lives
if I became a woodland gander
and you became a woodland goose,
and we had made our lonely nest
among some slender reeds.

From *A Manuscript of Ashes*

Antonio Muñoz Molina | Translated by Edith Grossman from Spanish (Spain)

It's the late sixties, the last dark years of Franco's dictatorship: Minaya, a university student in Madrid, is caught up in the student protests and the police are after him. He moves to his uncle Manuel's country estate in the small town of Mágina to write his thesis on an old friend of Manuel's, an obscure republican poet named Jacinto Solana.

The country house is full of traces of the poet—notes, photographs, journals—and Minaya soon discovers that, thirty years earlier, during the Spanish Civil War, both his uncle and Solana were in love with the same woman, the beautiful, unsettling Mariana. Engaged to Manuel, she was shot in the attic of the house on her wedding night. With the aid of Inés, a maid, Minaya begins to search for *Solana's lost masterpiece* Beatus Ille. *Looking for a book, he unravels a crime…*

EDITOR'S NOTE, HARCOURT

Antonio Muñoz Molina, the former director of the Cervantes Institute in New York City, was born in Jaén, Spain, in 1956, and currently divides his time between Madrid and Manhattan. He was trained as a journalist and art historian and is the author of numerous works of both fiction and non-fiction. He was twice-awarded Spain's Premio Nacional de Literatura (national literature prize), for *El invierno en Lisboa* (1987) and *El jinete polaco* (1991). The translation (by Margaret Sayers

Peden) of his novel *Sepharad* won the PEN/Book-of-the-Month Club Translation Prize in 2004. *A Manuscript of Ashes* (its original title is *Beatus Ille*) was his first novel, published in 1986, but translated into English only now, more than twenty years later. Yet it is in no way the work of a novice. The book is a stunning murder mystery and complex love story that takes place during the deadly time of the Spanish Civil War. The murder is truly mysterious, the historical evocations are powerful, the love story is compelling, and Muñoz Molina's writing is absolutely breathtaking. Translating the novel was challenging and exciting. I enjoyed the work from start to finish, and as a kind of bonus, the project also gave me the opportunity to work with Drenka Willen, a legendary editor at Harcourt.

EDITH GROSSMAN

Original text: Antonio Muñoz Molina, *Beatus Ille*. Barcelona: Seix Barral, 1986.

Beatus Ille

Primera parte, Uno

Ha cerrado muy despacio la puerta y ha salido con el sigilo de quien a medianoche deja a un enfermo que acaba de dormirse. He escuchado sus pasos lentos por el pasillo, temiendo o deseando que regresara en el último instante para dejar la maleta al pie de la cama y sentarse en ella con un gesto de rendición o fatiga, como si ya volviera del viaje que nunca hasta esta noche ha podido emprender. Al cerrarse la puerta la habitación ha quedado en sombras, y ahora sólo me alumbra el hilo de luz que viene del corredor y se desliza afiladamente hasta los pies de la cama, pero en la ventana hay una noche azul oscura y por sus postigos abiertos viene un aire de noche próxima al verano y cruzada desde muy lejos por las sirenas de los expresos que avanzan bajo la luna por el valle lívido del Guadalquivir y suben las laderas de Mágina camino de la estación donde él, Minaya, la está esperando ahora mismo sin atreverse siquiera a desear que Inés, delgada y sola, con su breve falda rosa y su pelo recogido en una cola de caballo, vaya a surgir en una esquina del andén. Está solo, sentado en un banco, fumando tal vez mientras mira las luces rojas y las vías y los vagones detenidos en el límite de la estación y de la noche. Ahora, cuando se ha cerrado la puerta, puedo, si quiero, imaginarlo todo para mí solo, es decir, para nadie, puedo hundir la cara bajo el embozo que Inés alisó con tan secreta ternura antes de marcharse y así, emboscado en la sombra y en el calor de mi cuerpo bajo las sábanas, puedo imaginar o contar lo que ha sucedido y aun dirigir sus pasos, los de Inés y los suyos, camino del encuentro y del reconocimiento en el andén vacío, como si en este instante....

A Manuscript Of Ashes

Part One, Chapter One

She closed the door very slowly and went out with the stealth of someone leaving a sick person who has just fallen asleep at midnight. I listened to her slow steps along the hallway, fearing or wishing she would return at the last minute to leave her suitcase at the foot of the bed and sit down on the edge with a gesture of surrender or fatigue, as if she had already returned from the journey she had never been able to take until tonight. When the door closed the room was left in darkness, and now my only illumination is the thread of light that enters from the hall and slides in a tapering line to the legs of the bed, but at the window there is dark blue night and through the open shutters comes the breeze of a night that is almost summer, crossed in the far distance by the whistles of express trains that travel under the moon along the livid valley of the Guadalquivir and climb the slopes of Mágina on their way to the station where he, Minaya, is waiting for her now without even daring to hope that Inés, slim and alone, with her short pink skirt and her hair pulled back into a ponytail, will appear at a corner of the platform. He is alone, sitting on a bench, smoking perhaps as he looks at the red lights and the tracks and the cars stopped at the end of the station and of the night. Now, when she closed the door, I can, if I want, imagine him for myself alone, that is, for no one, I can bury my face beneath the turned-down bedclothes that Inés smoothed with so much secret tenderness before she left and then, waiting in the darkness and in the heat of my body under the sheets, I can imagine or recount what happened and even direct their steps, those of Inés and his, on the way to their encounter and mutual acknowledgement on the empty platform, as if at this moment I had invented and depicted their presence, their desire, and their guilt.

She closed the door and didn't turn around to look at me because I had forbidden that, I only saw for the last time her slender white neck and the beginning of her hair and then I heard her steps fading as they moved away to the end of the hallway, where they stopped. Perhaps she put the suitcase on the floor and turned back to the door she had just closed, and then I was afraid and probably wished she wouldn't continue, but in an instant the footsteps could be heard again, farther away, very hollow now, on the stairs, and I know that when she reached the courtyard she stopped again and raised her eyes to the window, but I didn't look out because it was no longer necessary. My consciousness is enough, and the solitude, and the words I say quietly to guide her to the street and the station where he doesn't know how not to go on waiting for her. It is no longer necessary to write in order to guess things or invent them. He, Minaya, doesn't know that, and I suppose that some day he will succumb, inevitably, to the superstition of writing because he doesn't recognize the value of silence or of blank pages. Now as he waits for the train that, when this night ends and he arrives in Madrid, will have taken him away forever from Mágina, he looks at the deserted tracks and the shadows of the olive trees beyond the adobe walls, but between his eyes and the world, Inés and the house where he met her persist, along with the wedding portrait of Mariana, the mirror where Jacinto Solana looked at himself as he wrote a poem laconically entitled "Invitation." Like the first day, when he came to the house with the ill-fated melancholy of a guest who has recently gotten off the worst trains of the night, Minaya, in the station, still contemplates the white facade from the other side of the fountain, the tall house half-hidden by the mist of water that rises and falls back into the overflowing stone basin and sometimes goes higher than the rounded tops of the acacias. He looks at the house and senses behind him other glances that will converge there to expand its image by adding the distance of all the years that have passed since it was built, and he no longer knows if he remembers it himself or if rising in front of his eyes is the sedimented memory of all the men who have looked at it and lived in it since long before he was born. Undeniable perception, he thinks, amnesia, are gifts possessed completely only by mirrors, but if there were a mirror capable of remembering it would be set up before the facade of the house, and only it would have perceived the succession of what was immobile, the fable concealed beneath the stillness of closed balconies, its persistence in time.

At nightfall yellow lights are lit at the corners, which don't illuminate the plaza but only sculpt in the dark the entrance to a lane, brighten a patch of whitewash or the shape of a grating, suggest the doorway of a church in whose highest vaulted niche there is a vague Saint Peter decapitated by the rage of another time. The church, closed since 1936, and the headless apostle who still lifts an amputated hand in blessing, give the plaza its name, but the width of the plaza, never opened and very rarely disturbed by cars, is defined by the palace. The palace is older than the acacias and the hedges, but the fountain was already there when it was built, brought from Italy four centuries earlier by a duke who was devoted to Michelangelo, as was the church and its gargoyles black with lichens who when it rains expel water onto the street as if it were vomit. From the plaza, behind the trees, like a casual traveler, Minaya looks at the architecture of the house, still hesitating at the bronze doorknockers, two gilded hands that strike the dark wood and produce a somber, delayed resonance in the courtyard, under the glass dome. Marble flagstones, white columns supporting the glass-enclosed gallery, rooms with wooden floors where footsteps sounded as if in a ship's cabin, that day, the only one, when he was six years old and they brought him to the house and he walked on the mysterious parquet floor as if he were finally stepping on the material and dimensions of a space worthy of his imagination. Before that afternoon, when they walked through the plaza on their way to the Church of Santa María, his mother would squeeze his hand and walk faster to keep him from stopping on the sidewalk, trapped by the desire to stay there forever looking at the house, imagining what was behind the door that was so high and the balconies and the round windows at the top floor that lit up at night like the portholes of a submarine. At that time Minaya perceived things with a clarity very similar to astonishment and was always inventing mysterious connections among them that didn't explain the world to him but made it inhabited by fables or threats. Because he observed his mother's hostility toward that house he never asked her who lived there, but once, when the boy went with him to visit someone, his father stopped next to the fountain and with the sad irony that was, as Minaya learned many years later, his only weapon against the tenacity of his failure, he said:

"Do you see that big house? Well my cousin Manuel, your uncle, lives there."

From then on, the house and its mythological resident acquired for him the heroic stature of a movie adventure. Knowing a man lived in it who was inaccessible and yet his uncle produced in Minaya a pride similar to what he felt at times when he imagined that his real father was not the sad man who fell asleep every night at the table after making endless calculations in the margins of the newspaper, but the Coyote or Captain Thunder or the Masked Avenger, someone dressed in dark clothing and almost always wearing a mask who one day, very soon Minaya hoped, would come for him after a very long journey and return him to his true life and the dignity of his name. His father, the other one, who almost always was a shadow or a melancholy impostor, sat on one of the red easy chairs in his bedroom. The light had red tonalities when he closed the curtains, and on a pink background, as if in a camera obscura, small inverted silhouettes were outlined on the ceiling in the warm semi-darkness, a boy with a blue apron, a man on horseback, a slow cyclist, as detailed as a drawing in a book, who glided, head down, toward an angle of the wall and disappeared there behind the blue boy and the tenuous rider who preceded him.

Minaya knew something was going to happen that very afternoon. A truck had stopped at the door, and a gang of unknown, frightening men who smelled of sweat had walked calmly through the rooms, picking up the furniture in their bare arms, dragging the trunk that held his mother's dresses out to the street, throwing everything into confusion, shouting words to one another that he didn't know and that made him afraid. They hung a grapple and pulley from the eaves, ran a rope along it, stood on the balcony, attached the furniture he loved best, and Minaya, hidden behind a curtain, watched how an armoire that seemed to be have been damaged by those men, a table with curved legs where a plaster dog had always stood, his disassembled bed, swung over the street as if they were about to fall and break into pieces to the guffaws of the invaders. So that no torture would be denied him that afternoon, his mother had dressed him in the sailor suit she took out of the closet only when they were going to visit some gloomy relative. That's why he was hiding, aside from the fear the men caused in him, because if the boys on the street saw him dressed like that, with a blue bow on his chest and the absurd tippet that reminded him of an altar boy's habit, they would laugh at him with the uniform cruelty of their group, because they were like the men devastating his house, dirty, big, inexplicable, and wicked.

My God, his mother said afterward in the now empty dining room, looking at the bare walls, the lighter spots where the pictures had been, biting her painted lips, and her voice didn't sound the same in the stripped house. They had closed the door and were holding him by the hand as they walked in silence, and they didn't answer when he asked where they were going, but he, his intelligence sharpened by the sudden irruption of disorder, knew before they turned the corner of the Plaza of San Pedro and stopped at the door with the bronze door-knockers that were a woman's hands. His father adjusted the knot of his tie and stood straighter in his Sunday suit as if to recover all his stature, prodigious at the time. "Go on, you knock," he said to his mother but she refused, sourly, to listen to him. "Woman, you wouldn't want us to leave Mágina without saying goodbye to my cousin."

White columns, a high dome of red, yellow, blue glass, a gray-haired man who didn't resemble any movie heroes and who took him by the hand and led him to a large room with a parquet floor where the last light of the afternoon shone like a cold moon while a large shadow that may not belong to reality but to the modifications of memory inundated the walls supernaturally covered with all the books in the world. First he was motionless, sitting on the edge of a chair so high his feet didn't touch the floor, awed by the size of everything, the bookshelves, the large windows that faced the plaza, the vast space over his head. A slow-moving woman dressed in mourning came to serve them small steaming cups and she offered him something, a candy or a biscuit, using formal address with him, something that disconcerted him as much as finding out that the case that was so tall and dark and covered with glass was a clock. They, his parents and the man whom they had taken to calling his uncle, spoke in quiet voices, in a distant, neutral tone that made Minaya drowsy, acting like a sedative for his excitement and allowing him to retreat into the secret delight of looking at everything as if he were alone in the library.

"We're going to Madrid, Manuel," his father said. "And there we'll have a clean slate. In Mágina there's no stimulus for an enterprising man, there's no dynamism, no market."

Then his mother, very rigid and sitting next to him, covered her face with her hands, and it took Minaya a little while to realize that the strange, dry noise she was making was weeping, because until that afternoon he had never seen her cry. For the first time it was the weeping without tears that he learned to recognize and spy on for many years, and as he learned when his parents were already dead and safe from all misfortune or ruin, it revealed in his mother the obstinate, useless rancor toward life and the man who was always on the verge of becoming rich, of finding the partner or the opportunity that he too deserved, of breaking the siege of bad luck, of going to prison once because of a run-of-the-mill swindle.

"Your grandmother Cristina, son, she was the one who began our misfortune, because if she hadn't been stupid enough to fall in love with my father and renounce her family in order to marry him we'd be the ones living now in my cousin's palace and I'd have the capital to be a success in business. But your grandmother liked poetry and romanticism, and when my poor devil of a father, may he rest in peace and may God forgive me, dedicated some poems to her and told her a few vulgar clichés about love and twilight, she didn't care if he was a clerk at the Registry Office or that Don Apolonio, her father, your great-grandfather, threatened to disinherit her. And he certainly did disinherit her, just like in serialized novels, and he didn't see her again or ask about her for the rest of his life, which turned out to be short because of that unpleasantness, and he ruined her and me, and also you and your children if you have any, because how can I raise my head and give you a future if bad luck has pursued me since before I was born?"

"But it's absurd for you to complain. If my grandmother Cristina hadn't married your father, you wouldn't have been born."

"And you think that's a small privilege?"

A few days after the funeral of his parents, who when they died left him some family portraits and a rare instinct for sensing the proximity of failure, Minaya received a condolence letter from his uncle Manuel, written in the same very slanted and pointed hand he would recognize four years later in the brief invitation to spend a few weeks in February in Mágina, offering him his house and his library and all the help he could offer in his research on the life and work of Jacinto Solana, the almost unpublished poet of the generation of the Republic about whom Minaya was writing his doctoral dissertation.

"My cousin would have liked to be English," said his father. "He takes tea in the middle of the afternoon, smokes his pipe in a leather armchair, and to top it off he's a Republican, as if he were a bricklayer."

Not daring yet to use the knocker, Minaya searches in his overcoat for his uncle's letter as if it were a safe-conduct that would be demanded of him when the door was opened, when he crosses once more the entrance where there was a tile frieze and tries to reach the courtyard where he wandered that afternoon as if he were lost, expecting his parents to come out of the library, because the maid who had used *usted* with him led him away when his mother's weeping began, and he was possessed by the enduring fascination of the solemn faces that looked down at him from the paintings on the walls and by the light and the design of large flowers or birds formed by the panes of glass in the dome. At first he limited himself to walking in a straight line from one column to the next, because he liked the sound of his own methodical footsteps, and it was like inventing one of those games that only he knew, but then he dared to climb very silently the first steps toward the gallery, and his own image in the mirror on the landing obliged him to stop, a guardian or symmetrical enemy that forbade him to advance toward the upper rooms or enter the imaginary hallway that extended to the other side of the glass and where perhaps oblivion keeps several faces of Mariana that are not exactly the same, the print of Manuel when he went up after her in his lieutenant's uniform, the expression that Jacinto Solana's eyes had only one time in the small hours of May 21, 1937, unaware it was the eve of the crime, after being carried away by her caresses and tears on the grass in the garden and telling each other that guilt and the war didn't matter on that night when giving in to sleep would have been a betrayal of happiness.

In that mirror where Inés will not see herself again Minaya knows he will look for impossible traces of a boy dressed in a sailor suit who stopped in front of it twenty years earlier when a voice, his father's, ordered him to come down. In the courtyard he was taller than his cousin, and seeing his impeccable jacket and spotless boots and the opulent gesture with which he consulted the watch whose gold chain crossed his vest, one would have said he was the owner of the house. "If I'd had just half the opportunities my cousin has had from the time he was born," he would say, trapped between rancor and envy and an unconfessed family pride, because when all was said and done he too was the grandson of the man who built the house. He spoke of Manuel's errant ways and the lethargy into which his life seemed to have fallen since the day a stray bullet killed the woman he had just married, but his irony was never more poisonous than when he recalled his cousin's political ideas and the influence this Jacinto Solana had on them, a man who earned his living working for leftist papers in Madrid and who once spoke at a meeting of the Popular Front in the Mágina bull ring, who was sentenced to death after the war and then pardoned and who left prison to die in the way he deserved in a skirmish with the Civil Guard. And in this manner, ever since he had the use of his reason and the memory to recall sitting at the table after meals when his father made conjectures regarding senseless business deals and did long arithmetical operations in the margins of the newspaper, cursing the ingratitude of fortune and the insulting indolence and prosperity of his cousin, Minaya had formed a very blurred and at the same time very precise image of Manuel that was always inseparable from that one afternoon in his childhood and a certain idea of ancient heroism and peaceful seclusion. Now, when Manuel is dead and in Minaya's imagination his real story has supplanted the mystery of the gray-haired man who occupied it for twenty years, I want to invoke not his flight this evening but his return, the moment when he holds the letter he received in Madrid and prepares to knock at the door and is afraid it will be opened, but he doesn't know that returning and fleeing are the same, because tonight too, when he was leaving, he looked at the white facade and the circular windows on the top floor where a light is shining that illuminates no one, as if the submarine he wanted to inhabit in his childhood had been abandoned and was sailing without a pilot through an ocean of darkness. I'll never come back, he thinks, enraged in his grief, in his flight, in the memory of Inés, because he loves literature and the goodbyes forever that occur only in books, and he walks along the lanes with his head lowered, as if charging the air, and he comes out on the Plaza of General Orduña where there's a taxi that will take him to the station, perhaps the same one he took three months earlier when he came to Mágina to find in Manuel's house a refuge from his fear. It will be my pleasure to help you any way I can in your research on Jacinto Solana who, as you know, lived for a time in this house, in 1947, when he left prison, he had written, but I'm afraid you won't find a single trace of his work here, because everything he wrote before his death was destroyed in circumstances you no doubt can imagine.

Two Poems from *Black Thrush, Red Cherries*

Pēters Brūveris | Translated by Inara Cedrins from Latvian (Latvia)

Pēters Brūveris was born in Riga in 1957, and after graduating from the Department of Art and Culture at the Latvian State Conservatory worked as literary consultant to the journal *Latvijas Jaunatne* (Latvian Youth) and as director of literature for *Literatura un Maksla* (Art and Literature). He has published eight collections of poetry and four books for children. He's also written libretti and song lyrics as well as animation film scripts. Regarded as a leading poet in Latvia today, his poetry shows a breadth of experience and global scope, informed by his studies of and translations from Latin, Turkish, Azerbaijani, the Crimean Tatar language, Lithuanian, Russian, German, and Prussian. He has received the Klāvs Elsbergs Award (1987), the Preses Nams Award in Literature (2000, 2001), the Days of Poetry Prize (2001, 2005), the Award in Literature from the Baltic Assembly (2004), the Ojars Vacietis Poetry Prize (2006), and the Latvian National Prize for Best Book (2007). His poetry has been translated into Lithuanian, Russian, Swedish, German, Slovenian, Ukrainian, and English.

Pēters Brūveris sent me a manuscript titled *No One Answers Me*, written in the eighties and never published, as it was prohibited at the time, and two manuscripts of poetry published in the eighties—*Black Thrush, Red Cherries* and *Amber Skull*. Two poems are dedicated to my uncle, Vilis Cedrins, a political poet in Latvia during its brief years of independence. When the Russians invaded, my aunt fled to Stockholm in a fishing boat with one of their two young sons. My uncle planned to follow with their other son, but they were caught and placed in a prison camp in Riga. It was winter, there was no food, no heat, the camp was rife with disease—he died soon after being incarcerated. Pēters Brūveris reveres him as one of the three greatest Latvian poets and has written a footnote to the poems. As well as searching for a publisher for the books in translation, I am working on a manuscript of selections from Brūveris' latest three books, *Behind Glass, Flowers for Losers!*, and *The Landscape of Language.*

Original text: Pēters Brūveris, *Melnais strazds, sarkanie kirsi.* Riga: Liesma, 1987.

Atvadīšanās no sembas

Maz es atceros: gūlās migla
pār pļavu, egļu galotnēs
melnēja
aizmirstu varoņu vaibsti; pa taku
pārnāca neviens,
debesīs bez balss
riņķoja
mans liktenis, bet akas malā,
piesedzies ar dadža lapu,
tupēja krupis;
(tu vairs neatmodīsies—
staltradzis, kura rogos norietēja
tava Saule,
ir nomedīts, miris.)
tālumā noklusa ieroču šķinda,
melns kraukļa spārns

Parting from Semba

I remember little: fog lay
over the field, in fir crests
blackened
the features of forgotten warriors; down the trail
no one came,
in the skies voiceless
reeled
my destiny, but at the well's edge,
covered with a burdock leaf
a toad squatted;
(you'll no longer awaken—
the red deer, on whose horns
your Sun set,
is hunted down, dead.)
in the distance the clash of weaponry quieted,
a black raven's wing

aizklāja
manu sniegbālo roku,
aizdarīja man acis,
un es vairs neredzu,
ar ko es sarokojos—
ar miglu, ar nakti?
ar dzestru rupuču ķēniņa htonisko dvašu?

covered
my snow-white hand,
closed my eyes,
and I no longer see
what I'm wrestling with—
with mist, with night?
with a crystal tortoise king's chthonic breath?

Piesembas krasmalē

noklīdušu putnu bars
pirmssniega debesīs;
kas tur, selgas mijkrēslī,
vai smagas, piekrautas kuršu laivas
vai milzīgas zivju,
augšup nirdamas,
ēnas;
virs mums priedē šūpojas
mezglā sasējies ceļavējš;

ap mūsu pleciem
sarkandūla villaine; sarma
uz skropstām; pirkstu galos
mirušu putnu
ceļi;

tavās acīs tumšbrūni sveķi un unguņi;
manās—lūzdamas smilgas un nakts.

At Semba's Shore

flock of migrating birds lost
in skies before the first snow;
what's there, in the twilight of open sea,
is it heavily loaded Courlandish boats
or the shadows
of huge fish
rising;
above us in a pine sways
the tradewind tied in a knot;

about our shoulders
dull red shawl; frost
on eyelashes; on fingertips
dead birds'
paths

in your eyes dark brown resin and fires,
in mine—breaking spear-grass and night.

Poco-loco

Rodrigo Rey Rosa | Translated by Chris Andrews from Spanish (Guatemala)

Rodrigo Rey Rosa was born in Guatemala in 1958. Happily, he is not a stranger to readers in the English-speaking world. Three books of his early fiction were translated by Paul Bowles (*The Beggar's Knife*, *Dust on Her Tongue*, and *The Pelcari Project*); more recently, Esther Allen's translation of *The Good Cripple* (2004) was published by New Directions. Rey Rosa's first feature film *What Sebastian Dreamt*, based on his novel *Lo que soño Sebastián*, premiered at the 2004 Sundance Film Festival.

While not abandoning the short story, with which he began, Rodrigo Rey Rosa has also adopted ampler forms, particularly the short novel in short chapters. It would be misleading to call *Que me maten si…* (1997) or *Piedras encantadas* (2001) novellas: although short, they stake out large and complex imaginative territories. They seem to have been produced by drastic, ascetic editing of much longer texts. Rey Rosa's structural economies are reproduced in miniature at the level of the sentence; his precise, laconic style is the opposite of tropical luxuriance. The systematic and expert practise of the ellipse stimulates speculation on the reader's part without slackening narrative tension.

In a stimulating preface to *La orilla africana* (1999), the Catalan poet and critic Pere Gimferrer compares Rey Rosa's narratives to oriental and medieval tale-telling. Rey Rosa, he says, is a poetic narrator, not because of anything florid in his style, but because his stories seem to be self-sufficient, not pointing to any wider significance. In that respect, they are, according to Gimferrer, like the tales of the *1001 Nights*, and the opposite of Marcel Proust's giant novel (compared by the narrator to "the Arabian Nights [...] for a new age"), which is animated by a desire to weave significance back into experience through writing.

Fortunately, however, it is too soon to suppose that any characterization will apply to all of Rey Rosa's writing, for he continues to experiment, impelled by a salutary restlessness.

"Poco-loco" is taken from *Ningun lugar sagrado* (1998), a collection of shorter narrative texts mainly written in New York in the winter of 1997–1998. As the author explains in a prefatory note, "Poco-Loco" is "the simple retelling of a senseless crime that took place at 700 Ninth East Street," very close to where he was living.

Original text: Rodrigo Rey Rosa, "Poco-loco," originally published in *Ningún lugar sagrado*, pp. 15-25. Barcelona: Seix Barral, 1998.

Poco-loco

Así como Paracelso, el alquimista suizo, recorrió Europa de albergue en albergue hacia el final de su vida, pagando a los albergueros con monedas de oro que más tarde se convertían en conchitas de mar, Alicia Beerle, una chica de Zürich que fue a Nueva York a estudiar danza moderna, había soñado con errar de apartamento en apartamento por Manhattan, pagando a los propietarios con dinero encantado.

El taxi que tomó en el aeropuerto la dejó en el número 17 de Bleeker St. donde vivía Pati, una española diez años mayor que ella y amiga de amigos, quien le había ofrecido alojamiento por algunos días, mientras Alicia buscaba apartamento. Alicia tocó el timbre, y poco después Pati asomó la cabeza por la ventana de la nave del séptimo piso y dejó caer la llave de la puerta de la calle envuelta en un calcetín.

—Welcome to New York—le dijo Pati al abrirle la puerta, y Alicia entró en la nave casi sin aliento, a causa de la escalada. Así, comenzó a darse cuenta de que en el Nueva York de los artistas jóvenes las comodidades no sobraban; de que los edificios eran viejos y no era extraño que carecieran de ascensor, de que los muebles podían ser muy rústicos y las camas eran colchones extendidos en el suelo. También se enteró, pocos días más tarde, de que la hospitalidad duraba poco, y de que la manera más rápida de hallar vivienda en el excéntrico East Village era a través de los tablones de anuncios de algunos restaurantes y bares.

"Artista serio busca taller." "Cómo contactar a tu guía espiritual." "Clases de percusión." "Sacamos a pasear a tu perro." "Masajes a domicilio." "Vendo bicicleta." "Bailarina necesita compartir apartamento...."

Poco-loco

Like Paracelsus, the Swiss alchemist who, towards the end of his life, wandered from inn to inn across Europe, paying the innkeepers with gold coins that later turned into sea shells, Alicia Beerle, a girl from Zurich who went to New York to study modern dance, dreamed of drifting from apartment to apartment in Manhattan, paying the landlords with charmed money.

The taxi from the airport dropped her at number 17 Bleeker Street, where a Spanish woman called Pati lived. Pati was ten years older than Alicia, a friend of a friend, and had offered to put her up for a few days, while she looked for an apartment. Alicia rang the bell, and before long Pati leaned out of the window—her loft was on the seventh floor—and dropped a key to the street door, wrapped in a sock.

"Welcome to New York," said Pati as she opened the door of the loft, and Alicia walked in, somewhat breathless from the climb. Then and there she began to realize that young artists in New York did not necessarily enjoy all the comforts of modern life: the buildings were old, many had no lift, the furniture was often primitive, and mattresses rested directly on the floor. She also realized, a few days later, that hospitality soon ran out, and that the quickest way to find a place to live in the bohemian East Village was by looking on the notice boards in certain restaurants and bars.

Serious artist looking for studio space. How to find your spiritual guide. Percussion classes. We'll walk your dog. Massage: home visits. Bicycle for sale. Dancer looking for an apartment to share.

"Yes, Alicia speaking."

It was a guy with a southern accent, who had a two-room apartment to share. His name was Daniel and he suggested they meet the next afternoon at the Veselka, a Ukrainian restaurant.

"I'd be wary of sharing with a guy," said Pati later on, over dinner. "But of course it could turn out fine. Meet him and see what you think."

Alicia had taken a number of Martha Graham classes in Zurich, so she was familiar with the school's etiquette. She arrived fifteen minutes early with her monochrome unitard. The academy was an elegant four-storey brownstone in the Upper East Side, completely covered with ivy. After a brief interview with a severe-looking secretary, she was sent to an intermediate class in a salon on the first floor. To her surprise, almost all the other girls—there was only one boy—were Asian, and not at all friendly.

When she got back to the loft in Bleeker Street, Alicia went straight to the answering machine, but there were no messages for her or for Pati. So she made herself a light lunch and took a shower before going out to meet Daniel.

Perhaps Daniel Harkowitz would have been a different person if he had not been exposed to the concept of a personal, omnipotent deity, but from an early age he had been obsessed by the idea of the Christian God. "Religious delusions," said the forensic psychiatrists who examined him when he was ten, after he had tried to drown another boy of the same age during a baptismal ceremony on the banks of the Mississippi. However, instead of committing him to a psychiatric hospital, the judges at the Juvenile Court sent him to a reformatory, where he was kept until the age of fifteen.

There were times when he thought he was the Son of God and times when he thought he was Satan. There were also long periods during which he descended to the world of mortals and was subject to the laws of so-called reality. It was during one of these intervals that Daniel, who must have been about twenty-eight at the time, decided to move from Arkansas to New York City, which he did by hitching rides and jumping trains like a hobo.

For his first few months in New York he was more

or less homeless. He soon assumed the role of spiritual guide for one of the little groups of young nonconformists who were then camping in Tompkins Square Park. As winter approached he began to look for a place to live, since unlike most of the homeless people who spent summer in the square, he had no desire to lead a nomadic life and migrate south. With one of the girls he had met in the park, Mary Cohen, who was quite a successful beggar and an occasional prostitute, he took a two-room apartment at number 700 East Ninth Street, but they never mentioned this to their vagrant companions, so as not to make them envious.

For almost two years they shared the apartment. They lived in relative harmony, although they didn't see much of each other. Mary used to go to bed and get up very early, spending her days begging in the streets, while Daniel never rose before midday. In the afternoon he would go to the Tompkins Square library and assiduously read books about magic and religion, and at night he attended the cenacles regularly held in the park, where, for the benefit of a generally receptive audience, he set out his ideas on all manner of subjects and his plans for saving the world.

But one day in spring Mary disappeared without a trace or a word of explanation, and Daniel had a nervous breakdown. He didn't leave the apartment for fourteen days; he endured hunger and thirst; he grew very pale and thin. Two things were revealed to him during that crisis: he would have to find someone else to help him pay the rent; and he had to lay the foundations of the new religion that he would begin to spread—like Christ —at the age of thirty.

That was when Daniel began to appear in public with a little black chicken he called Poco on his shoulder, to which he spoke in a constant whisper. The Latinos who frequented the park gave him the nickname Poco-loco, by which he is still remembered in the neighborhood.

It was beginning to pour with rain when Alicia arrived at the restaurant. There was no one there waiting for her, but she sat at the bar and ordered a coffee.

"Hi," said Daniel and sat down on the stool next to her. He was wearing green camouflage pants and a little leather waistcoat—no shirt—against his grimy, pale, damp skin. He had a beard, long hair the color of dishwater and opaque eyes. The little black chicken was perched on his shoulder, with a red crest that looked like a punk hairdo.

"You're the one looking for an apartment? Sorry I'm late but…" He looked to the right and the left, and so did the chicken, pecking at its owner's ear and hair. "Poco's not allowed in here. Do you want to see it?"

When they went out into the street, it had stopped raining and the wet pavement was giving off a smell of tar. Daniel walked quickly with Alicia following two or three steps behind. They crossed Tompkins Square: a sound of drums and kids yelling, people throwing frisbees and walking their dogs. As they left the park, Daniel pointed out a three-storey building on Avenue B and said: "That's where Charlie used to live." They continued east along Ninth Street to number 700, an apartment building on the corner with Avenue C, opposite a vacant lot surrounded by a high, blackened wall covered with old posters, reminiscent of a Rauschenberg.

It was an iron-framed brick building dating from the middle of the nineteenth century, with masonry cornices and the standard fire escape on the outside. In the little entrance hall, up six decrepit steps, were three bicycles chained to an iron rail. Daniel's apartment was on the fourth floor; it didn't look out on the street but into a small interior courtyard, so there was little natural light. It was much smaller than Pati's loft, and once again Alicia thought that this was not the place for her. Daniel showed her one of the rooms—a dark cubicle where everything was covered with a layer of grey dust—then the bathroom and the kitchen, where the layer was composed of dust and black grease.

They stood facing each other in the little living room, and Alicia was impatient to be out of there.

"What do you think?" asked Daniel.

"I'm not sure; I'll need to think it over."

"The rent's good; I can't do it for less. You've got my number. Call me when you make up your mind, but don't take too long, OK?"

The next morning Alicia went to see another

apartment in Noho, two streets away from Bleeker Street. But it was more like a broom cupboard, and she rounded furiously on the agent who was trying to tell her it was a bargain. Two days later, after a series of similar let-downs, she rang Daniel and agreed to share the apartment with him from the following day, the first Thursday of the month.

Although she had prepared herself mentally, the sight of the place was just as dispiriting as before. Daniel greeted her coldly, strangely. After she had handed over the money—the first week's rent plus a bond—in exchange for the keys, he told her that he didn't use the telephone; if she wanted, she could keep the line, and pay the bill, but she'd have to get another handset, because the one that was there belonged to a friend and he had to give it back. Then he went out, saying he wouldn't be home until late.

As soon as she was alone, Alicia started cleaning. She worked for two hours in her room, then extended the operation to the living room, the kitchen and the bathroom. Having completed this task, she felt slightly better. She had filled three big bags with all sorts of rubbish. She would have to ask Daniel to follow certain basic rules, like cleaning up in the kitchen after meals, urinating *into* the toilet, and not letting Poco make a mess everywhere.

She was about to go into the bathroom and take a shower to wash off the sweat and the dirt, when it occurred to her to clean up Daniel's room as well. It had a sweetish smell; he was in the habit of burning incense. His bed, like hers, was a mattress lying on the floor. The window gave onto the fire escape, where Poco was standing on one claw, attached to the iron grille by a fine chain, staring off into the distance over a dark sea of rooftops under the evening sky. On the wall above the bed was a poster of Baphomet, the Judas Goat, and against the adjoining wall, on the ground, a row of old books. She decided it would be wiser to leave it all as it was. She went out of the room and shut the door.

After a long shower, she went down to the nearest store and bought coffee and a tub of yoghurt for dinner.

It would have been eleven by the time she got into bed, feeling tired. Now that it was cleaned and aired, her new bedroom no longer seemed a hostile place. It wouldn't be too hard to live there for a couple of weeks. If she wanted a place of her own, she'd have to work long hours just to pay the rent. When she fell asleep, at midnight, Daniel still hadn't come home.

Living with Daniel turned out to be easier than she had imagined, since they were hardly ever in the apartment at the same time, but she didn't feel at ease with him. She had the impression that he was doing his best to avoid her. On two occasions she saw him in the park, in the afternoon, with a group of young misfits who gathered under the trees as if to enact some scene from tribal life. Sometimes Daniel didn't come home until the morning, when Alicia was getting ready to go off to class. And in the afternoon, when she returned, Daniel was already gone or on the point of leaving.

Out of curiosity, Alicia had gone into Daniel's room two or three times and taken a look at some of his books: *The Autobiography of Anton S. Lavey; Real Magic* by Isaac Bonewitz; *The Ultimate Evil* by Maury Terry; *Paracelsus* by Robert Browning.

Even before opening the weekly paper she was depressed; she knew that the sort of apartment she wanted was beyond her means. She had two job offers, one as a waitress in a French restaurant, the other as a nanny for a German family, but even if she took both she wouldn't be earning enough to pay the rent. Nevertheless, she went through the advertisements for apartments to rent, column by column, noted telephone numbers and made up flyers.

The following afternoon, when she came back from her dance class, she found Daniel in the apartment. He was sitting on the battered black sofa, next to the telephone table, while Poco ran back and forth on the floor.

"There were calls for you," he said, by way of a greeting. "I didn't know you were looking for another apartment."

Alicia felt disproportionately guilty, as if she had committed some unforgivable offence. "Oh, yes. No, I didn't tell you," she replied. "I haven't seen you for a while…" She went to the door of her room, slipped the bag off her shoulder and let it fall onto the rumpled sheets of her bed. Then she crossed the living room to the kitchen, where she opened the fridge, took out a jug of water and poured herself a large glassful. She drank and looked at Daniel again. His gaze had followed her; it was hostile.

"When were you thinking of moving?" he asked.

Alicia put the glass down beside the sink.

"I don't know. I don't know if I'm going to move. I'm just looking, that's all."

Daniel lowered his eyes and started following Poco's movements.

"Do you have a complaint? Is something bothering you?"

"No, I really like it here," said Alicia. "It's just that I'd prefer to have a place of my own, you understand."

"The people who rang were talking about sharing, but never mind." He handed her a piece of paper, on which he had written down the names and numbers.

"You're free." Poco had stopped running around, and was now moving its head from side to side, as chickens do when they are scared. "But you're not free to go into my room and nose around."

"What?"

Daniel made a guttural noise and looked up at Alicia.

"Don't lie to me. I know you were in there. You left prints everywhere."

"Oh, but that was days ago." Alicia blinked. "I was going to sweep the floor. I'm sorry, I didn't mean to upset you."

She turned on her heel and was heading for her room when Daniel added, "And why were you snooping through my books?"

Alicia stopped in the doorway, confused, angry, feeling herself blush. She hung her head and took a breath before looking at Daniel again.

"I'm sorry," she said again. "I did have a look at your books. I couldn't resist."

"Poco, angel," said Daniel. "Come here."

The chicken obeyed: with two flaps it hopped into Daniel's lap and kept climbing until it came to rest on his shoulder. Then Daniel looked at Alicia again and said, "Bad, very bad," but as if he were not talking to her.

He turned to Poco.

"Ready?"

Alicia went into her room and shut the door. She locked it as quietly as she could, lifting the handle so the latch wouldn't make a noise, but she was sure Daniel had heard. Then, with a swarm of premonitions buzzing in her head, she sat down on the edge of the mattress.

Night fell, and Alicia, who had been sitting still for a long time, listening to the noises from the other side of the door—Daniel walking around in the living room, switching on the light, Was he washing dishes? Talking to Poco?—pushed her bag aside with one hand, smoothed the sheets and got into bed. She was scared, and cursed herself for having moved in there. She would leave tomorrow without fail; if Pati wouldn't have her, she'd go to a hotel.

It must have been around two when Alicia woke up.

She was still dressed; she felt hot and thirsty. The light in the living room was off and the apartment was quiet. She got up. She needed something to eat and drink. She went to the window, opened it wide and stood there listening to a police siren rapidly receding. A neighbor coughed. She went to the door, turned the key and stepped out. There was no one in the living room and the door to Daniel's room was shut. Gingerly, she made her way to the kitchen and switched on the light.

There was a big pot on one of the burners; her breath stopped dead. The pot contained Poco's entrails—intestines, liver, heart—floating in a swill of semi-congealed blood. Alicia's hand flew to her mouth; she looked away. Next to the sink was a black bowl full of black blood. She turned to the fridge and opened it. On the top shelf, sitting on a china plate, was Poco's head, with one eye open, staring indifferently; and underneath, on a chopping board, the plucked body, belly down. The chicken's white skin was covered with signs—crosses, circles, diamonds—drawn with blue ink. Alicia shut the fridge; she felt sick.

She went straight back to her room and locked the door behind her. It was the first time she had felt this kind of fear, like a living thing crawling all over her skin. She knew that her life was in danger and would be as long as she stayed in that apartment.

She looked at her watch: almost three o'clock. That didn't matter, she would leave straight away. She packed her bags and was ready to go in fifteen minutes. She didn't have her toiletries, which were in the bathroom, but she was prepared to leave them behind, and although she had thought about calling for a taxi, she decided not to: above all she wanted to avoid another encounter with Daniel. Once she crossed that threshold, once she was out of that apartment, the nightmare would be over and she would be safe.

She heaved the travel bag onto her shoulder, picked up her handbag, the empty sponge bag, and left the room. But there, between her and the front door, stood Daniel, arms crossed, staring at her.

"Have you seen Poco?" he asked.

Alicia started walking towards the door, making a detour to get around Daniel. But he moved quickly to block her way and shoved her back against the wall.

"You're crazy!" shouted Alicia. "Let me out!"

"Sure," he said, but he was holding a long-bladed bowie knife.

The legend that circulated around Tompkins Square, according to which Daniel fed his followers for several days on Alicia's flesh, may or may not be true. But Daniel himself was certainly the one who spread the rumor, and the police got wind of it. When they arrested him in his apartment, Alicia's head was still in a pot, in the freezer. Daniel did not deny his crime, but at the trial he declared that he had committed it in the name of God, who had ordered him to found a new religion and designated Alicia as a sacrificial victim. So he was found not guilty by reason of insanity and sent to a mental asylum in Syracuse, New York.

Two Poems from *L'Animal*

Emmanuel Moses | Translated by Marilyn Hacker from French (France)

Emmanuel Moses was born in Casablanca in 1959, the son of a French-educated German Jew and a French Jew: an historian of philosophy and a painter. He spent his early childhood in France, lived in Israel from the ages of ten to eighteen, and then returned to Paris, where he still lives. He is the author of six collections of poems, most recently *Figure rose* (2006), which received one of the 2007 annual Prix de poésie de l'Académie française, and of four novels. He is a translator of contemporary Hebrew fiction and poetry, notably of Yehuda Amichai. He also translates from the German and from the English, including poems by C. K. Williams and younger poets like the recent National Poetry Series winner

Donna Stonecipher. *Last News of Mr. Nobody*, a collection of Moses' poems translated into English by Kevin Hart, Marilyn Hacker, C. K. Williams and others, was published by The Other Press in 2005.

A polyglot whose experience of the world comes as much from travel and human intercourse as from books, from an interrogation of the past which coexists with his experience of the present, Emmanuel Moses is a kind of *poète sans frontières*. While some contemporary French poets eschew geographical specificity, a perennial subject of Moses' poems is the crossing and the porosity of actual borders, geographical and temporal. A (Proustian?) train of thought set in motion by the placement of

42   STRANGE HARBORS

a park bench, the stripe of sunlight on a brick wall, will move the speaker and the poem itself from Amsterdam to Jerusalem, from a boyhood memory to a 19th-century chronicle, from Stendhal to the Shoah. A subtle irony permeates Moses' work, even (or especially) at moments meant to be self-reflective or romantic, an irony applied to the events of history as readily as to the events of a single young or aging man's life. It is clear in Moses' poems as in his fiction that the macro-events of "history" are made up of the miniscule events of individual existence, or must be perceived as such to be understood. The breadth of the poet's reading and his intimate relationship with architecture, music and painting inform his work and populate it with unexpected interlocutors: Chopin, Buxtehude, Fragonard, Breughel—or a London barman, or a woman pharmacist in Istanbul.

The two sequences translated here are from a new, and not yet published, collection of poems entitled *L'Animal*. "Brandenburg Letters"—the state surrounding Berlin, identified with Bach—illustrates Moses' geographical and temporal jump-cutting, as its six sections (mirroring the concertos) move from childhood recollection to reflections on human communication to the abrupt, oblique description of a pogrom. "Riverbend Passage" is at once more lyric and linguistically ludic, though in a minor key and somber tone. Reading it, and, even more, translating it, I could perceive it as an homage to or dialogue with another Jewish poet without borders, Paul Celan.

Original text: Emmanuel Moses, "Lettres du Brandebourg" and "Passage du Méandre" from *L'Animal*. Paris: Flammarion, forthcoming in 2009.

Lettres du Brandebourg

Les cloches de l'existence ont sonné pour moi
il faut que je pousse enfin la petite porte
je connais ce jardin derrière la maison abandonnée
on y trouve du trèfle rouge et des brunelles
je me suis beaucoup promené en solitaire dans ses allées
pendant les années de légèreté
alors qu'entraîné par les nuages
je ne voyais d'autre sol que leur ombre

à ma soeur

Une fleur de silence comme décoration
entourée de claustras ouvragées de bonne foi
par les trous un gamin curieux voit des bouleaux/
vierge
qui cendrent un ciel dont se retire le jour

Brandenburg Letters

The bells of my life have rung for me
at last I'll have to push open the little door
I know this garden behind the abandoned house
you can find red clover there and small blue plums
I often walked alone down its rows of trees
during those years of lightness
when pulled along by clouds
the only ground I noticed was their shadow

to my sister

A flower of silence as decoration
surrounded by partitions carved in all good faith
through the openings a curious boy sees virgin
birches
which cinder a sky whose daylight is withdrawing

il marche pieds nus pour sentir la terre et l'herbe
plus tard on l'a conduit au bagne

❦

Mon ciel lavande enfermé dans un flacon
garde le secret que nous lui avions confié
la chaleur de ces jours-là est ailleurs maintenant
comme sont partis les torrents de lumière blanche
qui noient d'autres jardins où s'élève le désir
laissant les tables vides en bordure des pelouses

❦

A toi aussi — tu me pardonneras — G.S. 7 Anderson street Chelsea
j'écris un mot
et peu importe si tu ne réponds pas
puisque "ce qui a été ce cessera jamais d'être"
ainsi les hortensias deux maisons plus loin
auxquels tu devais beaucoup tenir
et l'été cette ombre verte orientale
qui enveloppait la rue presque tout le long

he walks barefoot to feel soil and grass
later he was taken away to jail

❄

My lavender sky closed in a perfume bottle
keeps the secret we confided in it
those days' heat is elsewhere now
just as the torrents of white light are gone
to drown other gardens where desire rises
leaving the tables empty at the lawns' edges

❄

To you as well—you'll pardon me—G.S. 7 Anderson Street, Chelsea
I write a note
and what does it matter if you don't answer
since "that which was will never cease to be"
thus the hydrangeas two houses over
of which you must have been very fond
and in summer that green eastern shadow
which enveloped almost the whole length of the street

Il partira sans que nous nous soyons compris
ou même reconnus
je ne sais pas pourquoi je te raconte cela
au lieu du rouge-queue sur le tronc du sapin
au début de l'après-midi
démesure de nos souffles
j'en ai pris conscience tout d'un coup
ni plus ni moins surpris que par une pluie d'été

Les tiens ont versé un sang violet
et l'usurier est devenu ange
dans le fossé s'accumulent des lettres d'amour
où les moribonds jouissent sans proférer un son
tandis que des diables célèbrent leurs noces

He will leave without our having understood
or even recognized each other
I don't know why I'm telling you about that
instead of the redstart on the pine trunk
in early afternoon
extravagance of our breathing
I noticed it all at once
not more or less surprised than by a summer shower

Your people shed purple blood
and the usurer became an angel
love letters pile up in the ditch
where the dying take their pleasure without making a sound
while devils celebrate their weddings

Passage du Méandre

Ne laissez pas l'homme en noir
m'emmener avec lui

     clarines/opéra

Il fut un temps où la misère s'allongeait sur moi
comme si elle voulait me réchauffer
vraiment elle me troublait l'esprit
j'étais
Biblique:

L'enfant craint l'eau et les abeilles
il regarde les hélicoptères treuiller des vaches
sa vie c'est toi
en bicéphale
et rebelote dans les alpages

Riverbend Passage

Don't let the man in black
take me away with him

      cowbells/opera

There was once a time when sorrow lay down on me
as if it wished to warm me
truly it troubled my spirit
I was
Biblical:

The child fears water and bees
he watches helicopters winch up cows
his life is you
bicephalous
in the mountain pastures again

De Malmaison à Malmort
l'homme me talonne
ne le laissez pas m'emmener sur son coursier noir
ou à bord du convoi noir
l'express intervital

Quand le soleil se couchera
je serai avalé
dissipé
volé en mille éclats de schiste
tu te souviens après la promenade
du silence heureux de la forêt

L'oiseau de quart
plantait des clous
les arbres morts étaient mon linge
pour la toilette des morts
je virerai au bleu de la vie
résolu comme l'abeille

From Badland to Deadwood
the man is on my heels
don't let him take me away on his black charger
or aboard the black convoy
the interlife express

When the sun sets
I will be swallowed
dispersed
blown away in a thousand shards of schist
after our walk you remember
the forest's joyful silence

The bird in quarter-view
planted nails
dead trees were my linens
for laying out the dead
I will turn towards life's blue
determined as a bee

Au pied de l'arbre foudroyé
déploration déploration
descente de croix mise en croix
l'unique oiseau pleure
le cheval bat du sabot
le père rêve de la nature
arrêtée

Dans les méandres intervitaux
l'épilobe s'élance vers le marcheur solitaire
ô sacrifice ô coutures
secrètes: conjonction

Ainsi vont les générations
et l'aigle immobile guette sa proie
jusqu'aux replis des pacages
clarines
reste enfant rétif
je—nous—nuages

At the foot of the lightning-blasted tree
lamentation lamentation
descent from the cross hung from the cross
the single bird weeps
the horse taps its shoe
the father dreams of nature
stopped short

In lives' riverbends
willowherb stretches out toward the man walking alone
o sacrifice, o secret
stitches: conjunction

Thus the generations continue
and the motionless eagle eyes his prey
down to the pastures' hidden nooks
cowbells
stay restless child
I—we—clouds

A l'infini
les nuages nous pressent et prient pour nous
la nature ne pèse rien
si un ange élève nos champs

L'âge au bout des méandres
quand se fait l'acte-miracle
de la procession—
éclosion

Le Roi me contait
cette histoire
le grand pondeur

Je l'écoutais
et sur le chemin du retour
je pleurais en silence
je croyais voir
des chevaux-fantômes

Clouds
press on us and pray for us forever
nature would weigh nothing
if an angel lifted our fields

Age, beyond all the bends
when the miracle of the
procession happens—
hatching, blossoming

The King told me
that story
he whelps litters of them

I listened to him
and on the way back
I wept silently
I thought I saw
ghost horses

j'entendais l'immensité du soleil
—un opéra—
j'étais magique métamorphosé
l'enfant sans repos

I heard the sun's hugeness
—an opera—
I was magical metamorphosed
the restless child

There's Lots to See

Agur Schiff | Translated by Jessica Cohen from Hebrew (Israel)

The short-story writer must rely to a great extent on readers' familiarity with settings and cultural references, absent the novel's more forgiving allowance for exposition. With this in mind, Agur Schiff's *Stories for Short Trips* plunges straight into dialogue and plot, with only the briefest of codes introducing us to the characters and locales. The translator, therefore, is called upon to retain this brevity of background and reproduce the fast-paced developments, with no time or space to spare for extraneous cultural explications. A number of qualities in Schiff's work both complicate this challenge and make it all the more seducing. With his artist's eye, Schiff's pointed physical descriptions of landscapes—urban, ru-ral, domestic and emotional—are immediately evoca-tive of a uniquely Israeli milieu. His protagonists, at first glance, are also instantly recognizable as the various Is-raeli archetypes they represent. Yet they are also much more than this, and the situations they encounter expose universal human weaknesses, blemishes, and aspirations. The themes in "There's Lots to See" appear in different guises in much of Schiff's work. His characters are often unhappy people who struggle with the incongruities be-tween their own observations and the way they are per-ceived by those around them. The stories depict relation-ships between lovers, friends, parents and strangers, and the protagonists also contend with a surprising number of animals—dogs, rabbits, pigs and sheep in this collection alone. An ever-present threat of violence permeates many of the stories, at times remaining dormant but menacing to the end, at other times erupting in disturbing ways.

Stories for Short Trips, Agur Schiff's second collection, was published in 2000, following his award-winning debut collection, *Dying Animals and Bad Weather* (1995). He has also published two novels, *Bad Habits* (2004) and, most recently, *What You Wished For* (2007), a biting political satire depicting two men's outlandish attempt to reconstruct a European *shtetl* on a hilltop in the occupied West Bank. Schiff was born in Tel Aviv in 1955 and is a graduate of St Martin's School of Art in London, where he specialized in animation. He won critical acclaim as a filmmaker before turning to writing. He is a senior lecturer at the Bezalel Academy of Art and Design in Jerusalem, and lives in Tel Aviv with his wife and two children.

Original text: Agur Schiff, "Yesh ma lir'ot" from *Sippurim le-nesi'ot ktzarot*. Tel Aviv: Hakibbutz Ham'eukhad, 2000.

יש מה לראות

זה היה יום באוקטובר, יום של אמצע השבוע, יום של כבישים מתפתלים. השמש הדביקה לגג־המכונית אצבעות לוהטות. ילדים ישבו עם ארגזי תפוחים בצדי הדרך.

בצהריים הגיעו למרגלות הצוק שעל מצחו התנוסס המבצר החרב כמו תרבוש מרופט. הם פנו שמאלה ונעצרו מול מחסום. איש בעל שפם פרום־קצוות בירך אותם בתנועת יד מחלון הבקתה שליד המחסום. "יש מה לראות," אמר בעל השפם, "לא תצטערו." ניר הושיט לבעל השפם שטר מחלון המכונית והאיש טמן בכף המחכה לעודף זוג כרטיסים, עלון מודפס ומטבעות. המחסום התרומם.

רוח יבשה הכתה באלונים הבודדים שעל מדרונות הבזלת. צרצרים התחרו זה בזה על תהודת הנקיק. במגרש החניה עמד רק אוטובוס אחד.

"איך קוראים למקום הזה?" שאלה עופרה.

"קלעת נמרוד."

הם עלו בשביל עפר, עברו את השלטים המספרים את תולדות האתר, ירדו במסדרון מקומר אל חדר שאיבד את

There's Lots to See

It was an October day, a mid-week day, a day of winding roads. The sun pressed its burning fingers on the car roof. Children sat along the sides of the road with crates of apples.

At midday they reached the foot of a cliff with a ruined fortress covering its forehead like a ragged fez. They turned left and stopped at a barricade. A man with a fraying mustache waved at them through the window of a hut. "There's lots to see," he called out, "you won't regret it." Nir handed the mustached man a bill through the car window and the man placed a pair of tickets, a printed brochure and some coins in his outstretched hand. The barricade rose.

A dry wind pounded the few oak trees dotting the basalt slopes. Competing cricket chirps echoed from the canyon. There was only one bus in the parking lot.

"What's this place called?" Ofra asked.

"Nimrod's Fortress."

They walked up a dirt road past signs recounting the site's history, down a curved passageway to a room that had lost its ceiling, and from there to a black vestibule with urine-smelling alcoves and light-seared rifle-slits. An earthquake had shifted the stones in the arches. That's what it said in the leaflet the mustached man had given them.

Nir pointed at the ceiling: "Look." She looked up. His hand longed to stroke her white neck.

A group of tourists crowded into the vestibule and Nir and Ofra slipped away and went down the steep staircase into the cistern. Algae-covered water stood there like a painted floor.

"It says there are salamanders here," said Nir, tossing a stone in.

The stone was swallowed up silently in the green surface.

The tourists walked by above them, glanced down, then disappeared. The whistling wind blew the echoes of their din outside.

"I would live here, if I could."

"Great idea."

"You'd probably come and visit me once in a while," said Nir.

She didn't answer.

"You'd come and visit me once in a while, wouldn't you?"

"Let's get out of here," said Ofra. "I'm sick of it, I'm thirsty and tired. Let's go back to the hotel."

She moved to the other side of the green pool and disappeared behind the wall. He followed her out into the sunlight.

"Wait up," he shouted, "why are you in such a hurry?"

Her slender silhouette skipped in front of his eyes as she walked down the path to the parking lot. He tripped on the slope and cursed.

Ofra was waiting for him in the shade under the snack-bar awning. The parking lot was empty.

"Got any money?" she asked.

He held out his wallet.

"Should I get you anything?"

"I'll share yours," he said.

Ofra bought a bottle of water and sat down on the edge of the bench. She peeled the plastic cover off the lid. Nir leaned against the awning pole and looked at her.

"What are you looking at me for?" she asked, irritated.

"No reason," said Nir.

Ofra held the bottle up to her mouth and emptied its entire contents down her throat. Then she wiped her lovely lips and put the empty bottle down on the cement floor. "Sorry," she said, "get another one."

But the snack-bar girl had already shuttered the iron doors over the counter and secured them with two large padlocks.

"Not many customers today, eh?" said Nir to the girl. Her cheeks and forehead were speckled with acne.

"Middle of the week," said the girl.

"What if we get thirsty again?" asked Nir.

"There's a water fountain up in the fortress," said the girl.

"Really?"

"Really."

"Well, maybe we'll go back there later to see the sunset," Nir said.

"You can't see the sunset," said the girl.

"Why not?"

"'Cause at five they close up the site." She walked away. Her high heels clicked down the road.

Ofra slumped with her back against the bench and closed her eyes. "I'm really sorry, but my fluids are depleted 'cause I got my period this morning." She spoke to the awning in a sleepy voice.

"Well at least we know you're not pregnant," said Nir angrily.

"Surprising," Ofra mumbled.

"You're trying to annoy me," said Nir, "but I won't let you, you won't be able to do it."

"Then how come you're getting annoyed?" asked Ofra with her eyes closed.

He bit his lips, walked out of the shade and looked at the fortress jutting out of a heap of black rectangles.

Ofra stood up and said, "Let's start heading back, if you don't mind."

"I like it here," said Nir.

"I'm leaving," said Ofra. She walked across the dusty gravel parking lot.

Nir caught up with her and grabbed her shoulder. "Then why did you even come with me? Why did you come here with me?"

Ofra tried to shake off his grip but his fingers dug into her hair, grasped her neck and pulled her to him. "Let me go," she said, "don't touch me. I don't like it when you touch me like that."

"Like what?"

"Violently."

He took hold of her chin and turned her face to him. Green spots burned in her eyes. "I don't like it when you touch me at all," she said quietly. "I can't stand the way you touch me, it gives me the chills."

His hand slid off her chin, lifted high above his head and then swung down on her cheek. Her head rocked sideways.

"Sorry," he said immediately. He couldn't stand her eyes when they turned back to him, and he looked away at the horizon, beyond the car roof. Smoke rose above the mountains.

"With you there's no difference between stroking and hitting," said Ofra. "It's the same hand connected to the same head."

"I said I was sorry," said Nir. "Why can't you forgive?" The slap stung the palm of his hand, and he slid it over his thigh as if removing a sticky residue.

"Because I can't stand your words either," said Ofra. "They're lying words, cheating words."

"I already said I was sorry. What more do you want?"

"I want to go to the hotel, pack up my stuff and go back to Tel Aviv."

Nir was quiet. Finally he said: "Okay. If that's what you want."

"That's what I want."

She walked around the car and opened the door.

"I hoped this would be like a second honeymoon," said Nir. "But what can you do. It's a lost cause."

"Yes."

"I'm sorry, Ofra," said Nir. "I want you to try and forgive me."

Ofra sat down in the front seat. She tore off a square from the roll of toilet paper crushed in the door compartment and blew her nose. Then she tilted the mirror and examined her lips.

Nir sat down next to her and put his hands on the wheel. "It was kind of your fault too," he said. "You drove me to it." Over the mountains, a new, thick plume of smoke was rising. Three small planes passed in the window like sparks flying from the sun, soared beyond the mirror and disappeared.

Ofra leaned her head back and closed her eyes.

"So that's that?" said Nir.

She said nothing.

"We can at least talk about it."

"I have nothing to say," said Ofra. "Please take me back to the hotel."

Nir's fingers drummed on the wheel. "I'm going to get a drink," he said suddenly.

Ofra sat up straight. "You're doing this to me on purpose, right?"

"I'm thirsty. The girl said there was a fountain up there."

"Get something to drink on the way, or just wait," said Ofra.

Nir stuck the key in the ignition and turned on the engine. "What can you do," he said.

A cloud of dust followed them until the wheels drove off the gravel onto the asphalt. Nir turned the windshield wipers on. The barricade appeared inside the wet arches. The mustached man came out to them. "How was it, guys?"

"We didn't see everything," said Nir.

"That's all right, come back another time." He bid them farewell with a salute.

The tires screeched when they made a right-turn. The fortress disappeared into the distance behind them.

"Calm down," said Ofra, but Nir picked up speed. "Do you want to kill me?!" she yelled.

Nir opened the window and leaned his elbow out. On his left, through the wind that slapped his face, village houses and rows of vines lined the foot of the hill. Down in the valley, fish hatcheries glistened among green and brown polygons, and on the horizon above the distant mountain ranges to the north, the pillars of smoke were frozen. The white stripe on the road flowed against Nir's eyes and alongside him, bending and straightening as he turned the wheel.

"Watch out!" Ofra screamed.

A herd of sheep was crossing the road. Nir slammed on the brakes. The car skidded and stopped at the bend with a screech. "You're such an idiot," said Ofra, "like a child." The stalled engine emitted a monotonous beep.

The shepherd, a tattered, white-haired man, looked disdainfully at the people in the car and turned back to his sheep, urging them on with gurgling and grunting sounds. The leaders of the herd stuck close to one another, taking small steps toward the incline on the other side of the road.

"You know what, Ofra?" Nir said suddenly. "Pay me back."

"What?" she raised her eyebrows theatrically.

Nir turned his head to one side to present her with his cheek. "Pay me back. Slap me as hard as you can."

"No, you pay me back," said Ofra. "Pay me back for all that time, those six years I wasted on you."

"Okay," said Nir. He remembered that he had a gun in the glove compartment. "Okay. I'll pay you back for everything. With interest and inflation. Every minute." The tumult of the sheep danced in front of his eyes.

"You know what?" Ofra said and smiled to herself. "It would actually be ideal if you lived in that fortress. Because then there wouldn't even be a remote chance that I'd run into you on the street." She giggled.

Nir leaned over to the glove compartment, careful not to touch her knees.

"What's that?" asked Ofra.

He removed the gun from its leather bag and cradled it in his hand.

"You don't know how to forgive, Ofra. You just don't know how to forgive."

He clicked the magazine into the butt and cocked the gun.

"What is this act?" asked Ofra.

Nir opened the door and walked out into the herd of sheep crossing the road.

"What are you doing, Nir?" Ofra shouted.

He lost his balance in the flowing herd, and grabbed onto the curls of a sheep.

"Piece of shit whore," said Nir. "I'll pay you back for every minute. Every minute, with interest on interest." He put the gun to the sheep's ear. "You whore!" he screamed and pulled the trigger.

The shot echoed back from the mountain. Blood spurted on Nir's arms. The parade of sheep became a galloping whirlwind and the dead sheep was carried along with her sisters until she finally fell on her back and was trampled.

Nir looked up and saw Ofra standing by the car door. "So what if I love you," he mumbled into the chaos of the frightened herd.

Then he saw Ofra marching up the road.

"Ofra!" he yelled after her. But she did not turn back, and he stood staring at her receding figure until the shepherd came up to him and said, "What did she do to you, my sheep?"

The last of the herd had crossed the road. Flies danced and buzzed around the carcass.

"Why did you kill her?" asked the shepherd.

"Don't know," said Nir. He took his wallet out of his pocket. "How much?"

"She was a good sheep," said the shepherd. "One-hundred shekels." A truck came around the bend.

Nir handed the money to the shepherd.

"Should I help you carry her to your car?" asked the shepherd. The truck honked as it drove by and left a long sooty trail behind it.

"No need," said Nir. He saw Ofra waving down the truck.

"Then what are you going to do with her now?" asked the shepherd.

"Don't know." The truck stopped and Ofra climbed up into the cabin.

"All right. Whatever you say," said the shepherd.

"I'm thirsty," said Nir.

"There's a snack-bar. There."

Nir turned around. The shepherd pointed at the fortress, now growing dark in the twilight. The distant truck climbed up the mountain, its headlights feeling out the bends as it went.

"Everything okay?" asked the shepherd.

"Yes, yes, everything's okay," said Nir.

The shepherd followed his bleating sheep and disappeared down the hill. The sunlight melted away over the mountains in the north. The wind rustled the woolen curls. Black blood congealed on the asphalt.

"So what if I love you," said Nir.

Two Poems from *Edward Hopper*

Ernest Farrés | Translated by Lawrence Venuti from Catalan (Spain)

A Spanish poet writes a book of poems on the paintings of a famous American artist. The painter enjoyed a central position in the artistic canon during his life, and now, with the international ascendancy of the United States, his influence stretches far and wide. The poet, however, chose to write in Catalan, a minor language brutally repressed under Franco's dictatorship and inevitably invested with nationalism. How does the poet treat the painter? With the deference commanded by prestige and power or an irreverence provoked by marginality and exclusion? What unique problems are posed by translating ekphrasis, the verbal representation of visual art? Most importantly, what intentions might guide a translation into English, the globally hegemonic language?

These questions have become my preoccupations as I translate Ernest Farrés' 2006 collection, *Edward Hopper*. Not only does Farrés boldly address an American icon, but in the opening poem he claims Hopper as his alter ego. "If Goethe was reincarnated in Kafka," he writes (in my version), "Hopper in a transmigration most apt / pulled it off in me." An ekphrastic text always transforms the visual work by inscribing a distinctively literary interpretation. Yet Farrés suggests a reading that is potentially interrogative. If Goethe, at once classical and romantic, metamorphosed into the absurdist Kafka,

Farrés might well be expected to give an ironic twist to Hopper's uncanny realism. The poet's intriguing analogy perfectly suits translation: the poems defamiliarize the canonical images with all the strangeness of the foreign. That the images are quintessentially American enables English to bring this effect back home, unsettling even while relying on the worldwide dominance of American culture.

Farrés' poems stage their emulative rivalry with the paintings by avoiding the gambit often preferred by Anglophone poets. His ekphrasis doesn't so much describe as speculate. He preempts any realist illusion by insisting on the artifice of the image, whereby shadows at dusk become "smudges," surreal colors are detached from the landscape, and a sunset is deepened with allusion. Occasionally the odd detail can be jolting: Catalunya, not Cape Cod, has "lizards." And Farrés' fondness for colloquial idioms invites the translator to vary current standard English, at points insinuating a linguistic difference through poetical, somewhat archaic, even ironic choices that Hopper himself might have made, like "take the glamour off," "hard by," and "dear departed." For the translator willing to listen to the Catalan, the subtlety of the poems is inspiring.

Original text: Ernest Farrés, *Edward Hopper*. Barcelona: Viena Edicions, 2006.

Railroad Sunset, 1929

Mentre declina el dia,
esmerlits núvols dissipant-se pengen
del cel policromat pel cantó de ponent.

El tros cobert de blau és d'un blau com Ulisses,
com l'atmosfera, com uns ulls turquesa
que s'alcen com el sol o com l'aigua que surt
de mare. Pel que concerneix el groc,
aquest té l'aura de les "grans conquestes."
És grogor de tremuja
de sembradora, de camp de rostoll
o de lluna rajant com mel de romaní.
A sota, la tonalitat vermella
podria evocar cirerers en flor,
maneres-porprades-de-ser-feliços
o peixos a l'aljub.

Railroad Sunset, 1929

While the day draws to a close,
gaunt, fading clouds hang
in the west corner of the polychrome sky.

The patch covered with blue is a blue like Ulysses,
like the atmosphere, like turquoise eyes
that rise like the sun or like water brimming
over. Respecting the yellow,
it is suffused with the aura of "great conquests."
It is the yellowness of a grain
hopper, a stubble field
or a moon flowing like rosemary honey.
Below, the shade of red
could evoke cherry trees in flower,
purple-ways-of-being-happy
or fish in a tank.

Es desfà el muntanyam
de l'horitzó en replecs
verdosos com la fullaraca o l'herba
del jardí i, a tocar,
es retallen les vies
fosforescents del tren
sobre un fons que, enfosquit
per la posta, és tan negre
com un mal averany
o com el grall d'un corb.

The mountain ridge dissolves
on the horizon in greenish
folds like fallen leaves or grass
in a garden and, hard by,
the phosphorescent train
tracks are limned
on a ground that, darkened
by the sundown, is as black
as an ill omen
or the deep croak of a raven.

Cape Cod Evening, 1939

Edward Hopper (1882–1967)

Cape Cod Evening, 1939

N'hi ha moltes més, de ganes de fer el mandra,
quan les clarors vesprals desmagnetitzen
els camins i la brossa i el bosquet,
donen al dia un to grisenc i esporguen
arestes i margallons.
                              Però cal,
que passi això, perquè tots, el marit,
la muller, el gos, s'estiguin en silenci
sense la pressió dels protocols,
sentin el vent xiulant entre les branques
o flairin una olor de figues.
                              Oh
com vagaregen els seus ulls (mig clucs,
en caure la tarda) pels regalims
de les soques, la brosta, les arrels,

Cape Cod Evening, 1939

You really feel like lazing around
when the twilight takes the glamour off
the paths, the underbrush, and the woods,
giving the day a grayish tint, pruning
ears of corn and palms.
                         This has
to happen for all of them—husband,
wife, dog—to fall silent
with no need of pleasantries,
listening to the wind whistle in the branches
or picking up the scent of figs.
                           And how
their eyes (half-closed, as night falls)
wander over the trickle
down the trunks, buds, roots,

les taques d'ombra, els formiguers, les pedres
i els llangardaixos dels camps del voltant.

Qui més qui menys fa els comptes de les ànimes
d'éssers pròxims que han pres, potser, la forma
de gotes tornassolades de pluja.

the smudges of shadow, ant hills, stones
and lizards in the fields all around.

Everyone more or less counts the souls
of the dear departed who take the form, perhaps,
of iridescent drops of rain.

Four Children, Two Dogs and Some Birds

Teolinda Gersão | Translated by Margaret Jull Costa from Portuguese (Portugal)

Teolinda Gersão (1940–) is a writer of short stories and novels. She has won many prizes in her native Portugal, and has appeared in English in *The Threepenny Review* and in the Norton anthology *New Sudden Fiction*. Her short stories, like all great examples of the genre, compress whole lives into a few telling pages. The story I have translated (from the collection *Histórias de ver e andar*) is one woman's account of trying and failing to be the consummate career-woman and the perfect wife and mother. It brilliantly blends the real and the metaphorical worlds and is written with wry humor.

Teolinda's stories are not, at first glance, difficult to translate. The syntax is simple, the vocabulary is that of everyday life. However, because many of the stories, including this one, are first-person narratives, what the translator must endeavor to capture is the tone of voice. The question I must keep asking myself is: How would this person speak if she were speaking in English? Once I've made an initial version, translating becomes largely a matter of ensuring that the flavor and swing of the words is entirely English. Seamus Heaney, I think, once commented that English is very much a verbal language, and I'm often struck by what a difference a verb can make in a translation. English is a very concrete, physical language and our seemingly limitless array of verbs is part of that physicality. A few examples:

(a) "Deixam sempre morrer as tartarugas, dão comida demais aos peixes e assustam-se com os gritos das araras."

becomes:

"People somehow always manage to kill off pet tortoises, they overfeed the fish and find squawking parrots positively alarming."

(b) "vi a água sair dos lados em jactos finos…"

becomes:

"[I] saw the water spurt out on all sides in a fine spray…"

Often a noun phrase becomes verbal:

"ouvia as patas leves dos cães…"

becomes:

"I could hear the dogs padding lightly around…"

These are just tiny examples of the translation process, but every translation is also a transformation, and that transformation takes place through such word-by-word choices. After twenty years as a translator caught between letter and spirit, I am more and more aware of the delicate balancing act translators have to perform every day.

Original text: Teolinda Gersão, "Quatro crianças, dois cães e pássaros" from *Histórias de ver e andar*. Lisbon: Dom Quixote, 2002.

Quatro crianças, dois cães e pássaros

É verdade que pus esse anúncio no jornal. Alguém que gostasse de crianças e estivesse disposto a cuidar dos animais. Cães e pássaros, nem toda a gente gosta de cães e pássaros. Embora talvez fosse mais difícil arranjar alguém para cuidar de tartarugas ou peixes. Ou pássaros grandes, como araras. Deixam sempre morrer as tartarugas, dão comida demais aos peixes e assustam-se com os gritos das araras. De modo que talvez eu não tivesse razão para me preocupar tanto. A final de contas cães e pássaros pequenos são animais muito comuns, que ninguém se espanta de encontrar na maioria das casas.

Mas eu estava muito cansada nessa altura, não tinha tempo de cuidar de nada, tudo se avolumava na minha cabeça como se fosse rebentá-la. Qualquer coisa, mesmo cães e pássaros, me parecia enorme e me esmagava.

Como se estivesse a viver um pesadelo. No escritório o trabalho era de loucos, saía sempre depois da hora e às vezes ainda escrevia cartas, mandava e-mails e fazia telefonemas em casa, sempre com uma horrível sensação de não conseguir fazer o principal. A mulher a dias saía antes de eu chegar, deixando as coisas apenas meio feitas, e a hora do jantar e dos banhos era um inferno, sem falar dos trabalhos de casa das crianças, que atropelavam os meus, ou dos meus, que também não deviam existir mas existiam, e atropelavam os delas. E no fim de tudo ainda era preciso dar comida aos cães, levá-los à rua e limpar a gaiola dos pássaros.

Claro que o Carlos não fazia nenhuma dessas coisas, embora me acusasse de trabalhar demais. Na verdade ele levava a mal que eu trabalhasse tanto, como se lhe fizesse uma ofensa pessoal. Não têm conta as vezes em que me arrependi de ter cedido às crianças…

Four Children, Two Dogs and Some Birds

Yes, I put the ad in the newspaper. Someone who likes children and would be prepared to look after a few pets as well. Only a couple of dogs and some birds, but then not everyone likes dogs and birds. Although it might have been even harder to find someone willing to take care of tortoises or fish. Or large birds, like parrots. People somehow always manage to kill off pet tortoises, they overfeed the fish and find squawking parrots positively alarming. So perhaps I needn't have worried. After all, dogs and small birds are the kind of perfectly ordinary creatures you might find in any home.

But I was *so* tired then that I didn't have time to look after anything; everything seemed to swell up inside my head until my brain felt as if it was about to explode. Everything, even dogs and birds, became an enormous, crushing weight.

It was like living in a nightmare. The amount of work I had to do at the office was absolutely crazy; I worked late every night, and even when I got home I'd sometimes still be writing letters, sending e-mails, making phone-calls, but always with a terrible nagging sense that I was never getting on top of the really important stuff. By the time I got home, our daily would have gone, leaving the housework only half-done, and supper time and bath time were utter hell, not to mention the children's homework, which got in the way of mine, *my* homework, which, of course, I shouldn't have been doing and which, in turn, got in the way of theirs. And then I still had to feed the dogs, take them for a walk and clean out the bird cage.

Needless to say, Carlos didn't do any of these things, although he was always accusing me of working too hard. In fact, he really resented me working so much, as if it were some kind of personal affront. The number of times I regretted having given in to the children and bought the animals. And the number of times, too, that I regretted having had the children. Not, of course, that I said as much.

Anyway, what was done was done, and now I just had to get on with it and look after the whole lot of them.

And then one day, I got really angry; enough is enough, I thought, and it was then that I decided to look for a live-in help.

A loving help, asked the concierge, puzzled, mishearing what I said when I informed her of my plan.

Exactly, I said, and the sooner the better. Today. Yesterday even.

Because I'll be dead tomorrow, I thought, starting up the car. Tomorrow I'll be dead.

But the days passed, and no help appeared. That was when I put the ad in. The animals were what worried me most. Any candidate for the job would be sure to change her mind when I told her, point-blank, even when everything was signed and sealed: Ah, by the way, we also have two dogs and some birds.

They'd be off like a shot. I was sure of it. Four children were quite enough. Four children, even without any pets, would discourage the very bravest of souls. Any normal person would keep a safe distance.

So I decided to be totally upfront about it and to explain the situation in the ad. Anyone who replied would know just what they were getting into and there'd be no nasty surprises. Not for me either.

In fact, I was very pleasantly surprised. After a few idiotic phonecalls and a number of unlikely candidates, I suddenly heard a calm, easy voice on the other end of the line. The owner of the voice even had a sense of humour, because I remember there was some silly misunderstanding or other, and she laughed, as if the whole thing was terribly amusing.

And when she arrived that same afternoon, I was able to confirm what the voice had promised: she seemed very confident and efficient. Cheerful too. She liked children and got on well with the dogs and the birds. She would take charge of everything, so I could dismiss the daily and finally get a little rest. I sighed deeply. At the time, I was just *so* tired.

At least I think that's how things happened. I lay down on the sofa and fell asleep.

I slept for weeks, months. I woke up and went to the office, or else didn't wake up at all and just slept day and night, with my eyes wide open. I would come home and go straight back to sleep, sitting on the sofa.

I was so very tired that things seemed to happen only vaguely and in the distance. I remember, for example, hearing the girl singing and the children laughing. I remember thinking that the house was finally clean and tidy. Hearing my children doing their homework in the kitchen and one of them asking: what's seven times four? And the girl answering: twenty-eight, and my son repeating: twenty-eight, and me thinking that that was also her age: twenty-eight.

And then another of my children started reading out loud, and I fell asleep, but I could still hear his voice.

Mine was an irresistible sleep that covered everything. I was simultaneously awake and asleep.

I could hear the dogs padding lightly around, the refrigerator purring, the tap dripping, a chair being moved. Through the open door I saw my youngest son climb onto a chair in the kitchen; he's going to fall, I thought, but made no move to help him; I saw him perched on the chair, saw him reach out his hands over the sink, turn on the tap, press the palm of his hand to the spout, saw the water spurt out on all sides in a fine spray soaking his face and clothes, not that he seemed bothered, because he laughed and stood on tiptoe in order to get still closer to the tap. Then the chair toppled noisily over and the child fell.

The sound of crying, then a warm, persuasive voice —it's all right, it's all right. The child, once he'd got up from the floor, his tears kissed away, snuggled up against the girl's slender form. Her tight-fitting apron tied around her waist.

Again the sound of the tap dripping, ping, ping, into the water in the sink.

One of the dogs comes over and sniffs me. Probably

checking to see that I'm not dead. One of my arms is hanging loose, almost touching the floor, but I don't move. The other dog comes racing up as well. Someone calls to them softly, grabs their leads and pulls them away, saying: Sh! Sh!

Ah, I think, they're going to take them for a walk. They disappear for a while, the dogs and the children. The front door bangs, there's the sound of the lift descending.

The sofa smells of dog. I can hear the birds chirping in the next room. It's late afternoon or early evening. Carlos will be home soon, I think, but I can't move. It may be Fall now, but it's still warm.

Time passes and now I hear footsteps again and noises around me. A child approaches and kisses me on the cheek. He puts his arms around my neck, and I know that it's my youngest son. Momma, he says, Momma. He shakes me, but I continue to sleep.

Finally, he leaves me and goes off in search of a book; he sits down on the carpet and starts to tear the pages. He picks up a glass, goes to the kitchen for water, places the glass on the table next to the sofa, kneels down on the floor, reaches out his hand for the glass and knocks it over. It'll mark the table, I think, because the water will leak onto the wood under the glass top. I think: Carlos will be furious when he finds out.

But when Carlos arrives home, he isn't furious, he doesn't even notice. He makes lots of noise with the kids, picks them up and hugs them. There's laughter, games, blindman's buff, perhaps, or hide-and-seek, with doors being opened and slammed shut again.

Now the children are doing their homework in their room, and he goes quietly into the kitchen, draws the girl to him and kisses her on the mouth.

And then they take each other by the hand and leave. They've packed their bags, and because it's now Winter, they've put on their overcoats and given the children anoraks to wear, as well as woolen gloves and hats. Carlos and the girl kiss each other again, furtively, on the lips, then close the door, and they all leave, without a sound, on tiptoe, taking the two dogs, both on the same lead, and carrying the birdcage.

Three Poems from *Newton's Orange*

Ewa Lipska | Translated by Margret Grebowicz from Polish (Poland)

Polish poet Ewa Lipska was born in 1945 and began writing in high school. She studied painting in college but decided that language was her proper medium and made her poetic debut in 1961. She worked as poetry editor for the publishing house Wydawnictwo Literackie for ten years. In 1975-76, she visited the University of Iowa as a fellow of the International Writing Program. She spent 1983 in West Berlin as a fellow of the Deutscher Akademisches Austausch Dienst. 1991 to 1997 was her longest period away from Poland, during which she lived in Vienna and worked at the Polish embassy as director of the Polish Institute. Since 1997, she has lived in Kraków but travels to Vienna often and is a member of both the Polish and the Austrian PEN Clubs. She is the recipient of numerous awards, including the PEN Club's Robert Graves award and the award of the city of Kraków, and a two-time nominee for the Nike, Poland's most prestigious award for a volume of poetry.

In a recent audio interview on her website, Ewa Lipska presents a curious inversion of the typical relationship between author and translator. Rather than the translator's existence depending on the author's, it is the author whose being is sustained by her translators. "They are our heroes. Without them, we don't exist. I have been saying lately that in my next incarnation I will be a pianist!"

Indeed, Lipska's work has matured in a deep and complex relationship to translation, since the 1979 collection of her work in Hungarian. At present, there are over twenty foreign language collections. But in spite of her adaptability to languages like Catalán and Albanian, translation remains something enigmatic and powerful for Lipska, something she never takes for granted. These days, she describes translators as mad acrobats facing impossible tasks. "They really are like circus performers walking a tightrope... There are many formulations that are simply untranslatable, that do not work at all in another language... To translate poetry, to suffer like that, and then to get paid peanuts for it, one must be insane."

The irreducibly hyphenated nature of the translation relation (linguistic and cultural), the undecidability of the conjunction/separation between author and translator, the curious "us" it engenders—these are among the central problems of her work. The present poems are from her most recent volume, *Newton's Orange* (2007), where she continues to trouble these themes in the context of unified Europe, of globalization, democratization, today's wars and legacies of wars.

Original text: Ewa Lipska, *Pomarańcza Newtona*. Warsaw: Wydawnictwo Literackie, 2007.

Plama

Podczas kontroli bezpieczeństwa
na lotnisku w Zurychu
stoję w magnetycznej bramce.

Na nic wykrywacze metali.

Moje drobnoziarniste tomy wierszy.
Arkusze ekspresyjnej blachy. Chromowana ironia.
Brzęczące żetony aforyzmów
przesuwają się powoli jak cierpliwość.

Terrorystyczne myśli
nie intrygują nawet
podejrzliwej chwili.

The Stain

During the security check
at the Zurich airport
I stand in the magnetic gate.

Useless metal detectors.

The fine-grained volumes of my poems.
Sheets of expressive steel. Chrome irony.
The buzzing pages of aphorisms
move along slow as patience.

Terroristic thoughts
don't provoke so much
as a suspicious moment.

Patrzymy sobie w oczy
jak metal z metalem.

Co może wiedzieć maszyna
o zagadce poezji
która mnie rozwiązuje
już sześćdziesiąt lat.

Na ekranie skanera
to zaledwie
plama
po prawej stronie.

We gaze into each other's eyes
like metal at metal.

What can a machine know
about the poem puzzle
that has been solving me
for sixty years now.

On the screen of the scanner
it's merely
a stain
on the right hand side.

Psi Węch

Gaśnie poezja
w niepiśmiennym śnie.

Przez ziemską galerię
przetacza się „Wóz z sianem" Hieronima Boscha.

Przegrany anioł
stoi na skraju autostrady.
Paruje silnik.

O siano
oparta władza.
Kwitnie
przydrożna gawiedź.

The Canine Sense of Smell

Poetry was extinguished
in its illiterate sleep.

"The Haywain" by Hieronymus Bosch wobbles
across the earthly gallery.

A defeated angel
stands at the edge of the highway.
An engine steams.

The leadership leans
against a haystack.
A mob blooms
on the shoulder.

Diabeł rozdaje
odtwarzacze MP3.
Kusi nas muzyką.

Boskie szatańskie sztuczki.
Ponad chmurami Chrystus.
Na drodze pielgrzym.

Między nimi psi węch
i posępna cisza.

The devil hands out
mp3 players.
He tempts us with music.

Divine satanic little arts.
Christ above the clouds.
A pilgrim on the road.

Between them the canine sense of smell
and a grave silence.

Pomarańcza Newtona

Grawitacja

Spotykam ją
na rynku starego miasta.
Może starożytnego Rzymu.

Nosi na sobie
zjadliwy kolor
przegranego życia.

Wyśmiewa sekundy.
Pestki słonecznika.

W militarnej pamięci
przechowuje zmianę warty.

Newton's Orange

Gravity

I run into it
in the old market square.
Maybe in ancient Rome.

It wears
the sarcastic color
of a wasted life.

It laughs seconds out loud.
Sunflower seeds.

In its military memory
it harbors a changing of the guard.

Przykłada ucho do wilgotnej ziemi.
Tyka puls nadchodzących wskazówek.
Kiedy leży
pod roztargnionym drzewem
spada na nią
człowiek.

It presses its ear against the moist ground.
The ticking pulse of approaching clock hands.
As it lies
under a ravaged tree
a human
falls on it.

From *Vilnius Poker*

Ričardas Gavelis | Translated by Elizabeth Novickas from Lithuanian (Lithuania)

There's something compellingly real, even if sometimes compellingly obnoxious, about Ričardas Gavelis' world, or shall I say worlds? And this in spite of what some take him for—a fantasy writer. The pudding he serves up in his novel *Vilnius Poker* (*Vilniaus pokeris*) is such a mix of literary genres that it's impossible to classify it, and in fact, the text switches pace so frequently that I found the work of translating, which some would find really rather tiresome with its reading, reading and re-reading of the texts, not in the least bit tedious. And despite the gruesome excursions into Lithuania's troubled past, the rampant and all-too-plausible paranoia, and the constantly palpable degradation of the Soviet experience, I still cannot get past the line: "That's no ordinary frog—that's Madam Vargalienė" without laughing.

Published at the beginnings of Lithuania's stirrings for independence, this book caused quite a stir, and its instant best-seller status brought Gavelis fame as a controversial writer. Gavelis' love for his country and the city of Vilnius is merciless and devastatingly critical, another aspect that makes him so difficult a read. However, he has always had his readers, those who could see that beyond the insane fantasies, frank sexuality, and wildly contradictory narration there lies an unblinking examination of the human condition. His writing style is pithy, precise and carefully crafted; when revising, I was often surprised to discover how the more I whittled out of the English sentence, the closer it got to the Lithuanian original. Word order in Lithuanian is quite flexible, a tool Gavelis uses with great care. His vigorous use of tense and person, unusual vocabulary, word plays, intertextuality, and word inventions all require particular attention. Martynas' grammatical error in the quote from Wilde's "The Ballad of Reading Gaol" is a typical Gavelis prank.

Gavelis (1950–2002) is the author of seven novels, three short story collections and several plays; he also wrote on economics and politics. He graduated from the University of Vilnius with a degree in physics, a background that would find expression in his novels not only in their obsession with time and space, but in their remarkably structured composition. The complete English translation of *Vilnius Poker* will be published in the spring of 2009 by Open Letter Press. What follows is the opening narration of two of the four poker players of Vilnius.

Original text: Ričardas Gavelis, *Vilniaus pokeris*.
Vilnius: Vaga, 1989, second edition.

Pirma dalis: Jie

Vytautas Vargalys   197… metų spalio 8-oji diena

Siauras plyšys tarp dviejų daugiaaukščių, spraga aklilangiais inkrustuotoje sienoje: keista anga į kitokį pasaulį—anapus laksto vaikai ir šunys, o šiapus—vien tuščia gatvė ir vėjo genami dulkių tumulai. Pailgas veidas, atgręžtas į mane: siauros lūpos, kiek įdubę skruostai ir tylios akys (turbūt rudos)—moters veidas, pienas ir kraujas, klausimas ir kančia, dievybė ir ištvirkimas, daina ir nebylystė. Senas laukinių vynuogių stiebais apraizgytas namas sodo gilumoje, kiek dešiniau padžiūvusios obelys, o kairėje—geltoni nesugrėbti lapai, jie plevena ore, nors plonytėliausios krūmų šakos nė nevirpteli…

Toks atsibudau šį rytą (*kažkurį* rytą). Kiekvieną mano dieną pradeda skausmingai ryškių vaizdų atsklanda, jos negali pramanyti ar pats pasirinkti. Ją parenka kažkas kitas, ji suskamba tyloje, perveria smegenis dar neatsibudusiam ir vėl dingsta. Bet neištrinsi jos iš atminties, ta nebyli preliudija nuspalvina visą dieną. Negali nuo jos pasprukti—nebent suvis neatsimerktum, nepakeltum galvos nuo pagalvės. Tačiau visad paklūsti: praveri akis ir vėl matai savo kambarį, knygas lentynose, ant fotelio sumestus rūbus. Nejučia klausi, kas parinko dermę, kodėl galėsi sugroti savo dieną tik taip, o ne kitaip? Kas yra tasai slaptas prapulties demiurgas? Ar pats renkiesi bent melodiją, ar tavo mintis jau supančiojo Jie?

Labai svarbu, ar ryto vaizdiniai tėra prisiminimų sąraizga, kitados regėtų vietų, veidų, įvykių pablukę paveikslai, ar jie pasirodo tavyje pirmą sykį. Prisiminimai spalvina gyvenimą daugmaž įprastomis spalvomis, o nebūtais reginiais prasidėjusi diena esti pavojinga. Tokiomis dienomis atsiveria pragarmės ir ištrūksta iš narvų žvėrys. Tokiomis dienomis lengvesni daiktai sveria daugiau už sunkesnius…

Part one: They

Vytautas Vargalys   The eighth of October, 197…

A narrow crack between two high-rises, a break in a wall encrusted with blind windows: a strange opening to another world—on the other side children and dogs run about, while on this side—only an empty street and tufts of dust chased by the wind. An elongated face, turned towards me: narrow lips, slightly hollowed cheeks and quiet eyes (probably brown)—a woman's face, milk and blood, questioning and torment, divinity and depravity, music and muteness. An old house, entangled in wild grape vines, in the depths of a garden; a bit to the left dried-up apple trees, and on the right—yellow unraked leaves; they flutter in the air, even though the tiniest branches of the bushes don't so much as tremble…

That was how I awoke this morning (*some* morning). Every day of mine begins with an excruciatingly clear pictorial frontispiece, you cannot invent it or select it yourself. It's selected by someone else, it resonates in the silence, pierces the still sleeping brain and disappears again. But you won't erase it from your memory; this mute prelude colors the entire day. You won't escape it—unless perhaps you never opened your eyes or raised your head from the pillow. However, you always obey: you open your eyes and once again you see your room, the books on the shelves, the clothes thrown on the armchair. Unconsciously you ask, who's chosen the key, why can you play your day in just this way, and not another? Who is that secret demiurge of doom? Do you at least select the melody yourself, or have They already shackled your thoughts?

It's of enormous significance whether the morning's images are just a tangle of memories, merely faded pictures of locations, faces or incidents you've seen before, or if they appear within you for the first time. Memories color life in more or less familiar colors, while a day that begins with nonexistent sights is dangerous. On days like that abysses open up and beasts escape from their cages. On days like that the lightest things weigh more than the heaviest, and compasses show directions for which there are no names. Days like that are always unexpected—like today (if that was today)… An old house in the depths of a garden, an elongated woman's face, a break in a solid wall of blind windows… I immediately recognized Karoliniškės' cramped buildings and the empty street; I recognized the yard where even children walk alone, play alone. I wasn't surprised by the face, either, *her* face—the frightened, elongated face of a madonna, the eyes that did not gaze at me, but solely into her own interior. Only the old wooden house with walls blackened by rain and the yellow leaves scattered by a yellow wind made me uneasy. A house like a warning, a caution whispered by hidden lips. The dream made me uneasy, too; it was absolutely full of birds, they beat the snowy white drifts with their wings, raising a frosty, brilliant dust, the dust of moonlight.

How many birds can fit into one dream?

Part two: From the mlog

Martynas Poška   October 14–29, 197…

Everyone keeps asking me about Vytautas Vargalys. But what can I say? "The man has killed the thing he loved, and so the man must die."

It started raining just after the sobering events of the garden. Vilnius is steeped in mud that reeks of sulfur. It's as if the devils of hell had spat up everything. Picking linden blossoms in the city's environs has been forbidden for quite some time now, unless you have an urge to slowly poison yourself. When civilizations die, even nature opposes it. Whether I want to or not, I feel like I am the chronicler of the dying Lithuanian civilization.

My height—five foot seven and a half inches. I cut my hair in a crew cut. At some point this hairstyle will return victorious to Vilnius' streets, so I'll instantly become fashionable.

I know, I know, no one is interested in my person. No one inquires about how I'm doing. Everyone just keeps asking about Vytautas Vargalys.

News bulletin: I don't get myself involved in mysterious and horrible incidents. I don't cut people to pieces. I can't even manage to write a real log. I call it the mlog—after my name.

And what ought I to write in it now?

What can I say about Vytautas Vargalys? Probably very little of the real truth: I don't know what he was like in his childhood. You can't really say much about a person if you don't know what he was like as a child. It's hard for me to talk about him. I can only relate facts with certainty. Probably that's appropriate when writing a log. But writing an mlog?

When I'm asked if he could murder someone, and so brutally, too, I answer honestly: no, he couldn't murder anyone.

But I'm quiet about something else: he could have murdered his mania, his past, his menacing ghost. That's just what he did. But I don't say this to anyone and won't. They wouldn't understand. They just hunger for bread and circuses. They hunger for blood, someone else's, of course. To them, Vargalys is nothing more than a live sensation. A monster of Vilnius, stirring up our sleepy anthill in the blink of an eye.

I'm not interested in ants. I'm interested in humans. And I haven't known that many of them. They're so rare.

I state with conviction: Vytautas Vargalys was a human.

Metamorphosis

Tedi López Mills | Translated by Wendy Burk from Spanish (Mexico)

The day I met Tedi López Mills, we saw desert mistletoe. Kore Press had just published *While Light Is Built*, her first collection in English. Now the Mexico City-born poet, author of ten books and winner of the Octavio Paz Foundation's inaugural fellowship, was in Tucson reading for The University of Arizona Poetry Center. In "Snow," a poem included in *While Light Is Built*, López Mills writes, "I have never seen mistletoe." Here we were in the Sonoran Desert, mistletoe clinging to nearly every mesquite and palo verde in view. How could we not go see?

In the Internet age, I can find a photo of mistletoe (or anything else) with one click. It's rare to see something for the first time, as on that day, unmediated by flat screen. Yet I associate first sight, unfiltered and just-unveiled, with López Mills' work. She says as much in her poem "Garden," describing the titular garden: "the one I saw first / is the one I still see, / the one I summon."

Frances Sjoberg, in her introduction to *While Light Is Built*, comments that "Tedi López Mills is in the midst of an ongoing conversation." This statement captures my experience of translating the first sights of López Mills' poetry. I converse with—interrogate, really—her images:

"What are you? What am I seeing?" What, for example, is the "semispherical window in the mist" that opens the poem "Metamorphosis"? A break in the clouds? An airplane window?

The beauty of the Internet age is the ease of conversing with both poem and poet. I can email López Mills to ask "What am I seeing?" Interestingly, she favors a literal approach: the semispherical window in the mist is… a semispherical window in the mist. That's what she wrote; that's what it is. This challenges me, an associative and emotional translator. To be true to sight, but still find my point of connection, I look for a visual image that encapsulates the poem's emotional register. For example, in "Metamorphosis," it is the "curved city" with its "watery passage / in the coming and going of light" that first let me into the poem. I saw the city in my mind, rising up from the river like one of Calvino's invisible cities, awash with eerie, eruptive light. Then I truly saw it: the whole poem, as if for the first time. *The one I saw first is the one I summon.*

Original Text: Tedi López Mills, "Metamorfosis," from *Horas*. México DF: Trilce Ediciones, 2000.

Metamorfosis

Un cristal semiesférico en la bruma
       cubre esta tierra de humo,
esta tierra de lava
       en los costados del monte,
esta arenisca, esta ladera,
       este cimiento de roca.

Hubo una ciudad curva en el flanco,
       hubo un paso de agua
en el trasiego de las luces.
       Y era arroyo, era río,
era el cuerpo disperso
       luego de haber fundido
la piel con la grava
       y no dejar nada escrito,
o no decirlo a tiempo.

Metamorphosis

A semispherical window in the mist
      covers this land of smoke,
this land of lava
      on the mountainside,
this sandstone, this hill,
      this rocky foundation.

There was a curved city here,
      there was a watery passage
in the coming and going of light.
      And it was a stream, a river,
a body scattered
      after skin
melted with gravel
      leaving nothing written down,
or nothing said in time.

Figúrate el pergamino,
las manos entumecidas
        por la inercia del silencio,
la palabra matizada por un nombre,
        tu nombre,
los papiros arrinconados
        tras el polvo y la batalla minúscula
de mantenerse nítido al menos
        sin riesgo de borrar el mensaje,
tu mensaje:
        no fue nada,
plomo y nervios,
        esa escritura detrás de la reja,
ese residuo desigual de una muralla.

De quién sería el rasgo;
         la grieta lírica no fue tu cara,
no fue el dedo en tu boca
        la señal de una sustancia interna;

                Imagine the parchment,
hands numbed
                by the inertia of silence,
word qualified by a name,
                your name,
papyrus forgotten
                after the dust and the minuscule battle
to at least retain clarity
                without risking the message,
your message:
                it was nothing,
just lead and nerves,
                that writing behind the fence,
those unequal remains of city walls.

Whose features could they be;
                the lyric fissure was not your face,
the finger in your mouth was not
                a sign of internal substance;

adentro nunca existió,
       afuera se oía sólo una voz,
sólo el destello en tus rocas,
       luego la carne del risco
que fuiste,
       la gruta debajo del mundo
donde caímos,
       caíste,
la astilla clavada tan hondo
       ¿fue una liturgia
aunque no hubiera sangre?

inside never existed,
          outside, only a voice was heard,
only your glinting rocks,
          then the flesh of the cliff
you used to be,
          the cavern below the world
where we fell,
          you fell,
the splinter stuck so deep—
          could it have been
a bloodless liturgy?

The Girl Who Was Born from an Apple

Matilda Koen-Sarano and Ester Navon Kamar | Translated by Trudy Balch from Ladino (Ottoman Turkey)

This folktale from Matilda Koen-Sarano's *Konsejas i konsejikas del mundo djudeo-espanyol* (roughly "Stories, Fables, and Fantasy Tales from the Judeo-Spanish World") is but a taste of the rich genre of Sephardic Jewish oral literature in Judeo-Spanish, also known as Ladino. Koen-Sarano, born in Italy to Turkish Sephardic parents in 1939 and a resident of Israel since 1960, now devotes her life to storytelling and to collecting Sephardic folktales.

A Jewish woman born in Italy to Sephardic parents from Turkey? What better metaphor for the development of Judeo-Spanish! When the Jews were expelled from Spain ("Sepharad" in Hebrew) at the end of the 15th century, many went to Ottoman Turkey. There they continued to speak Spanish, maintaining 15th-century vocabulary and pronunciation while sprinkling it with Turkish, Greek, Hebrew and other languages. Over time they emigrated, especially when the Ottoman empire collapsed after World War I. Though in Ottoman days the language was written in the Hebrew alphabet, Judeo-Spanish today is usually written in phonetic transcription. In the system used here, the letter "j" signifies a "zh" sound, like the "s" in "pleasure."

Translating this story involved a number of intriguing cultural and linguistic issues. For example, language that now sounds archaic yet still conversational, with a lively folktale style. I decided to use a folktale/fairytale style in English ("Once there was…"), sprinkled with slightly archaic-sounding phrases or words such as "I can no longer abide…," "…have befallen me," "suckle," and "And so it was…." The story opens with a childless couple in which the husband "loved his wife so much that he did not want to divorce her." Readers of the original would understand that the husband did not mind not having children—often grounds for divorce. My solution was "loved his wife so much that he did not want to divorce her because of it."

"When we were children, our mothers put us to bed to these *konsejas*," Koen-Sarano writes in her introduction (my translation). "Our parents used these *konsejas* to teach us about good behavior and good deeds…. In these *konsejas* we find words that explain why life is the way it is…."

Original Text: Matilda Koen-Sarano and Ester Navon Kamar, "La ijika nasida de una mansana" from *Konsejas i konsejikas del mundo djudeo-espanyol.* Jerusalem: Kana, 1994.

La ijika nasida de una mansana

Avía un zug ke no tinía kriaturas, i él la kiría tanto bien a la mujer, ke no la kijo kitar.

Un día pasó por la kaye uno ke vindía fruta, diziendo: "Vendo mansanas pele. Ken las kome keda prenyana. Tengo dos sortes: una para ijiko i una para ijika!"

Vino la mujer, merkó dos mansanas, las metió debasho del kavesal i hue s'echo a durmir. Vino a echarse el marido, vido una koza dura debasho el kavesal. Metió la mano, topó una de las mansanas, disho: "Mira ermozura de mansana!" i se la komió.

Pasó tiempo, de día en día se le sta unflando el pie de mala manera, i le sta dueliendo.

Sta diziendo: "Kualo tengo? Kualo es esto?" Ya se metió unguente, ya s'izo banyo, no le valió.

Disho un día: "Day! Y m'izi bizer de la vida i kare ke miri kualo ay ariento. Si es materia, ki salga!"

Tumó una navajika i se hue al kampo. Se asentó debasho de un árvol i avrió el pie. Sta mirando: salió una manizika. Avrió mas, salió un pieziziko. Fin a ke salió una ermozura de ijika.

"Uay!" disho, "Komo de veruensa! Kualo van a dizir por mi? Ke de mi pie nasa una kriatura? No puede ser!" Tomó, la emburujó bueno a la kriatura, la deshó ayá en basho i fuyó.

Pasó por ay un roé kon los kodreros, los metió a komer yerva. Vido ke un kodrero le sta mankando de vez en kuando. Se hue a bushaldo, vido ke este kodreriko avrió los piezes i sta dando a mamar leche a una kriatura.

Disho: "Komo de maraviyas ay al mundo! Ke le kuadre al kodrero a dar a mamar a esta kriatura!"

Tomó la kriatura, l'emburujó bueno i la yevó…

The Girl Who Was Born from an Apple

Once there was a couple who had no children, but the husband loved his wife so much that he did not want to divorce her because of it.

Then one day a man came down the street selling fruit, saying: "Magic apples for sale! Whoever eats them will become pregnant. I have two kinds: one for a boy, and one for a girl!"

The woman bought two apples, put them under her pillow and went to sleep. When her husband came to bed, he saw something hard underneath the pillow. He stuck in his hand and found one of the apples. "Look, what a beautiful apple!" he said, and he ate it all up.

As time went by, his foot swelled more and more horribly with each passing day, and it hurt very much.

"What's wrong with me?" the man said. "What could be happening?" He rubbed ointment on his foot and soaked it in water, but it didn't do a bit of good.

One day he said, "Enough! I can no longer abide life like this. I must see what is inside my foot. If it's pus, then let it come out!"

He took a penknife and set off for the fields, and then he sat down underneath a tree and cut open his foot. As he looked, a little hand came out. He made the cut bigger, and out came a tiny foot. Finally out came a beautiful little girl.

"Oh!" he said. "How can this shame have befallen me! What will people say? A daughter born from my foot? It cannot be!" He took the little girl, wrapped her up tightly, left her there under the tree, and ran away.

Then a shepherd came by with his sheep, and he put them out to pasture. From time to time he noticed that one was missing. He went to look for it, and saw that the sheep had spread its legs and was suckling a baby girl.

"Miracle of miracles!" the shepherd said. "To think it would occur to a sheep to suckle a little baby!"

He picked up the little girl, wrapped her well, and took her to the royal palace. "Here, I found this baby underneath a tree," he said to the king. And then he told the king how the sheep had suckled her.

And so it was that the baby stayed in the royal palace and grew up there, and she became a beautiful young woman and married the prince. And her father never learned what had become of her.

TOLD BY ESTER NAVON KAMAR
(1906–1998), JERUSALEM

FACING The first four paragraphs of "The Girl Who Was Born from an Apple" as written in *solitreo*, the cursive Hebrew script traditionally used to write Ladino by hand.

Two Poems by Nuala Ní Dhomhnaill

Translated by Ivy Porpotage from Gaelic (Ireland)

Nuala Ní Dhomhnaill is a writer who is not only committed to the Irish Gaelic language and Irish folklore, but to taking both back for women. She is one of the most prominent poets writing in the Irish Gaelic language and has been translated by English-speaking Irish poets such as Seamus Heaney, Paul Muldoon, and Medbh McGuckian. The poems I have translated are drawn from Ní Dhomhnaill's collections, *The Water Horse* and *Pharaoh's Daughter*.

I translated the poems under the tutelage of poet Myra Sklarew, former professor of Literature at American University. I was also fortunate to obtain some feedback on one of my translations from Dr. Coilin Owens, Professor Emeritus of English at George Mason University.

I approached the translation process like one might approach a puzzle, one for which I was neither sure I had all the pieces, nor sure I could fit them together properly if I did. Although I had Robert Bly's *The Eight Stages of Translation* and notions from George Steiner's *After Babel: Aspects of Language and Translation* in my head throughout the translation process, I found learning about Ní Dhomhnaill's influences to be most helpful in translating her work. Some of my biggest "finds" during the translation process were drawn from Irish folklore and Celtic mythology.

Sometimes as writers we crawl so deep inside ourselves that we forget what we have in common with other writers. Embarking on this translation effort reminded me how universal the written word really is, whatever the language. It allows us to connect with ideas that haven't been spoken and heard. Translating Ní Dhomhnaill's work has been particularly rewarding to me because it reminds me that even when we cannot put words to our own thoughts, there are ways to convey meaning by reflecting on literature and history. For example, in "Ceist na Teangan," Ní Dhomhnaill expresses her strong connection to the Irish language by recalling the story of Moses. This leads me to think that nothing is untranslatable. It may just be a matter of finding the right language and images to express it, and perhaps a very talented writer like Ní Dhomhnaill to do so.

Original text: Nuala Ní Dhomhnaill, "Oileán"
from *Pharaoh's Daughter* (1993); and
"'Fhir a' Bháta" from *The Water Horse* (2000).
Both published by Wake Forest University Press.

Oileán

Oileán is ea do chorp
i lár na mara móire.
Tá do ghéaga spréite ar bhraillín
gléigeal os farraige faoileán.

Toibreacha fíoruisce iad t'uisí
tá íochtar fola orthu is uachtar meala.
Thabharfaidís fuarán dom
i lár mo bheirfin
is deoch slánaithe
sa bhfiabhras.

Tá do dhá shúil
mar locha sléibhe
lá breá Lúnasa
nuair a bhíonn an spéir

Island

Your body is an island
asleep on the ocean floor.
Your limbs blow in a white sheet
above a sea of gulls.

Your brow is a fountain
of blood and honey.
I go to your fountain
during a sweltering heat
and drink to ease
my fever.

Your eyes gleam
like a mountain lake
on a fine Lammas day
when the Leo sky

ag glinniúint sna huiscí.
Giolcaigh scuabacha iad t'fhabhraí
ag fás faoina gciumhais.

Is dá mbeadh agam báidín
chun teacht faoi do dhéin,
báidín fiondruine,
gan barrchleite amach uirthi
ná bunchleite isteach uirthi
ach aon chleite amháin
droimeann dearg
ag déanamh ceoil
dom fhéin ar bord,

thógfainn suas
na seolta boga bána
bogóideacha; threabhfainn
trí fharraigí arda
is thiocfainn chughat
mar luíonn tú
uaigneach, iathghlas,

sparkles in the water.
Your eyelashes are reeds
sprouting along the edge.

And if I had a boat
to take me to you,
a findrinny boat,
its top above ground
its bottom below,
but for a lone feather
white-backed, red
making music
on deck for me,

I would raise
the graceful bow
to plough through
the high sea
and come to you
as you lie
lonesome, green-meadowed,

'Fhir a' Bháta

Nuair a d'fhágais
do churachán coirt bheithe
taobh leis an dtoinn
ag cur ceangal
lae is bliana uirthi
i gcás ná beifeá riamh uaithi
ach aon uair a' chloig amháin,

do chuiris dhá théad i muir
agus téad i dtír uirthi
in áit nach raibh
tonn dá bualadh,
gaoth dá luascadh,
grian dá grianscoltadh
nó fiú préacháin an aeir
ag déanamh caca uirthi.

The Boatman

When you left
your little boat of birch bark
beside the wave
placing a spell
of a day and a year on her
even though you were away
for only one hour,

you put two ropes in the sea
and one rope on land
in a place where she would not be
beaten by waves,
swayed by the wind,
burned by the sun
or shit on by
crows in the air.

Tú féin a bhí tar éis
í a thógaint ó bhonn,
ag saoirseacht ar bhalcóin
do thí samhraidh,
ag fí meathán agus tuigí dearga
i bhfráma naomhógach.
D'aithníos láithreach tú
is thuig an gaol
nach féidir a shéanadh
a chuirfidh orm an doras a dhúnadh
amach anseo
le hosna thuirseach.

Is dála an phailnithe tré uisce
a imíonn ar lus na ribin
mar a scaoiltear aníos na blátha fireann
ó íochtar an duibheagáin
is go snámhann na staimíní lastaithe
le gráinníní troma pailín,
iad á gcumhdach ó uachtar an uisce

She was yours alone after
she rose up from the foundation,
crafted on the balcony
of your summer house,
weaving saplings and red skins
in the shape of a little boat.
Your appearance deceived you
and you knew the relationship
that could not be denied
set at the door, shut
out here
with a weary sigh.

And the pollen meets the water
traveling on the ribbon plant
as the male flower sprouts up
from the lowest depths
and the stamen swim charged
with small grains of pollen,
they are protected from the surface of the water

ag báidíní beaga pontúin
na bpiotal,

seol, a bhuachaillín,
seol do bhád
isteach sna trí phiotal gléineacha
atá im' chroí im' lár.

by little pontoon boats
of petals

sail in, young man,
sail your boat
in among the lucent petals
which is my heart, my very core.

From *The Brothers of Consolation*

Patrick Besson | Translated by Edward Gauvin from French (France)

Born in 1956 to a Croatian mother and a Russian father, the unpredictable Patrick Besson burst precociously onto the scene with his first novel in 1974. He has since produced, with the same dizzying force that informs his headlong prose, more than twenty books, including his Croatian saga *Dara* (Albin Michel), winner of the 1985 *Grand Prix du Roman de l'Académie Française*. The *Prix Renaudot* and *Populiste* followed ten years later, for his novel *Les Braban* (Albin Michel, 1995), on which occasion he was dubbed "The Prince of Paradox" for shocking the world on separate occasions by championing Mike Tyson and the Serbians. He is a communist by upbringing, polemicist by practice, prodigy by talent, and *enfant terrible* by trade.

Les Frères de la Consolation is a feast of a novel. Originally published in 1998, this Goncourt-nominated epic takes its title from Balzac's *L'Envers de l'histoire contemporaine*. It sweeps readers from Greece through the glittering Paris of Sand, Musset, Gay, and Dumas, of cholera and the barricades, of Gavroche and Vidocq, all the way to America, across the turbulence of the mid-19th century, trailing headlong the adventures of two Serbian brothers: Miloš the warrior and Srdjan the poet.

Their cousin Milena, married to the Count de la Renardière, loves Miloš. Srdjan loves Milena, and Miloš is a force of nature. Besson's cavalcade of notables includes the real, the imagined, and the larger than life, who have since become legend. A portrait of society sparkling with deceit, in which every line of dialogue is an enticement or a riposte, a quip or a barb, *Les Frères de la Consolation* presents a world dizzy with vice and glory, whose only grace is transience.

Besson's swift, decisive prose seems at first to render on his characters gadfly judgments that, on closer examination, turn out to be profound: a look, a line of dialogue, a facial feature seized upon and made, by his knack for turning a phrase and then reprising it to provide a key to character in all manner of contexts. Miloš *is* his mustache, Srdjan his height, Nerval his melancholy, and Hugo his obsession with money; each mention of a defining trait adds a layer of reality and animation to figures fictional and historical alike.

This early chapter was translated in a fit of enthusiasm long before finishing the novel, or even reaching a point that gave me a sense of how it played into the story. Pages go by—in fact, the whole first part of the book—without indication that it is more than the episode it seems. It's a testament to the novel's roominess and impact that long after a series of Parisian set-pieces have shuffled Miloš' marriage from the reader's mind, it returns to lodge stubbornly in the plot, a obstacle to the characters' happiness.

What drove me to render Besson's chapter in English was the rhythm of his sentences—the same clip at which I imagined his horseback hero galloping along; his cynical wit; and his ultimately large-hearted chivalry, like that of a slightly soured Dumas. Here is a novel of, as Jean-Rémi Barland would have it, "princely melancholy." *Ko traži nać će.*

Original text: Patrick Besson, *Les Frères de la Consolation*. Paris: Éditions Grasset, 1998.

Les Frères de la Consolation

Miloš refusa d'accompagner Macropoulos à Athènes. Il toucha sa dernière solde—vingt thalers—, avec laquelle il acheta un petit cheval maigre, mais lui-même n'était pas gros. Il dit adieu au général et aux officiers, fit une longue tournée parmi la troupe, récita une prière sur la tombe d'Hamilton. Il pensait que c'était à ce moment-là qu'il ne pourrait plus contenir ses larmes. Il se trompait: il ne se mit à pleurer qu'après avoir quitté Thèbes et ensuite, jusqu'à la mer, une ou deux fois par jour.

Il était si bouleversé et surexcité qu'il se disait qu'il ferait le trajet Thèbes-Belgrade d'un coup, sans manger ni dormir. Il traversa Livadia, Elazia et Lamia sans les voir. Il ne sentait ni la chaleur ni la soif. Il avait juste l'impression que son cheval faiblissait sous lui. Il le vendit sur le marché de Karpenissi, la moitié du prix qu'il l'avait acheté. Il n'avait jamais eu le sens des affaires et, en plus, avait beaucoup esquinté l'animal en ne lui laissant aucun repos et en le nourrissant et l'abreuvant à peine. De Karpenissi, il rejoignit Komboti, puis Arta. Dommage que Macriyannis ne fût pas avec lui: que de fois l'avait-il entendu vanter les paysages de sa chère Roumélie! Montagnes massives couvertes de maquis, ruisseaux limpides, sentiers mélancoliques bordés de bruyères arborescentes. Miloš aimait bien les Rouméliotes: ils commençaient par l'accueillir avec un fusil, puis, après qu'il avait prononcé le nom de Macriyannis, le lui offraient, avec l'hospitalité pour le restant de ses jours. Miloš se contentait d'un bol de soupe et d'une meule de foin. Il n'avait envie de causer avec personne, de boire avec personne, d'être heureux avec personne. La seule chose qu'il voulait c'était arriver à Belgrade. Il savait que dans sa ville il trouverait quoi faire de sa vie, maintenant qu'il n'avait plus la guerre…

The Brothers of Consolation

Miloš refused to accompany Macropoulos to Athens. He took his final pay—twenty thalers—and with it bought a skinny little horse. But he himself was not a large man. He bid the general and the officers goodbye, made his rounds with the troops, and said a prayer over Hamilton's grave. He'd believed that moment would find him at last unable to hold back his tears, but he was wrong: he didn't cry until he'd left Thebes and, thereafter, all the way to the ocean, once or twice a day.

He was so overcome and distraught that he resolved to ride from Thebes to Belgrade without stopping, eating, or sleeping. He passed unseeingly through Livadia, Elazia, and Lamia. He knew neither heat nor thirst. He had only an impression that his horse was flagging beneath him. He sold it in the market at Karpenissi at half the price he'd bought it for. He'd never had a head

for business and moreover, had worn the animal down greatly, giving it no rest and hardly any food or water. From Karpenissi, he moved on to Komboti, then Arti. A pity Macriyannis wasn't with him: how often Miloš had heard him praise the landscape of his dear Rumelia! Massive mountains covered in scrub, limpid streams, melancholy trails bordered by branching heather. Miloš loved the Rumelians: they greeted him with a rifle which, once he'd uttered Macriyannis' name, they offered him, along with hospitality for the rest of his days. Miloš made do with a bowl of soup and a haystack. He did not want to speak, drink, or be happy with anyone. The only thing he wanted was to reach Belgrade. He knew that in his own city he'd find something to do with his life, now that he no longer had the war to fill it. He wanted to see Srdjan, his wonderful younger brother, gifted in all things, kind, cheerful, and who, it was said, now stood taller than Miloš by a good half a head, so greatly had he grown in eight years.

The village of Margariti was deserted when, on the 27th of September, 1829—a date he would have reason to remember for the rest of his life—Miloš rode in. He knocked on the doors of the first few houses, without success. If the town had succumbed to an epidemic of cholera, he would have seen the bodies. Suddenly, from nowhere, came a young man walking toward him, deathly pale, his forehead dripping sweat. Miloš hailed him, but the man gave no answer. This would normally have caused the Serb to draw his knife and demand an explanation, but he saw that the man was not in a normal state. He vanished into the countryside. More and more intrigued, Miloš turned for the church—made of wood, that it might be quickly taken down in case of a Turkish raid—where the villagers were gathered around a young woman, calm of face and cold of eye, in a bridal gown. She was the first to see him. One by one, the Rumelian faces turned toward him and he readied himself, as usual, to say the magic word—"Macriyannis"—when the young woman stepped up to him and asked if he would like to marry her. He said yes. She took him by the arm and led him into the midst of the Rumelians, presenting him, with a threatening air, as her husband-to-be. The villagers muttered, looking away from him. He understood nothing and couldn't care less. All he knew was that if he married this girl, they'd give him a good dinner. He was hungry that day. It had taken crossing all of Greece on foot from east to west for him to recover his appetite. He also reflected that he had not made love since the death of his wife five years, eight months, and thirteen days ago.

A Rumelian about fifty years of age, decked out in the traditional *fustanella* and an ad hoc mustache, approached Miloš. The Serb knew him at once to be the father of the bride, for the two had the same eyes. The man asked him who he was and where he came from. Miloš told him. The man asked him if he wanted to marry his daughter. Miloš said yes. The man asked him if he would settle in Margariti after the marriage. Miloš said no. Whereupon the man blessed him and asked if he wished to bathe before the ceremony. Miloš considered it, then accepted. He might have been wedded just as well unwashed, but knew that one ate better after a bath. One of the bride's brothers led him to the family house. On the way over, he asked Miloš to recount the battle of Navarin. Miloš promised he would do so during the banquet. He gave himself over to two young and sturdy serving girls who scrubbed him thoroughly, shaved him, lotioned him, powdered him, and dressed him in a handsome new Rumelian suit. He knew then that he was about to marry well, someone of his own class. He resisted the temptation to ask the servants what was going on. The war was over, he had no more need of tidings. Another thing not clear to him was whether the father wanted him to leave Margariti before or after the wedding night. He would have preferred after, but if it had to be before, he'd make no fuss. He was convinced that he would never again in his life make a fuss.

He had not noticed, earlier, that his bride was so beautiful. She had a broad, domed forehead full of gentleness and innocence. Her father's eyes, of course: long, golden, sharp. A tidy little nose, a tidy little mouth, and perfect teeth. What surprised him was her age: at least twenty-six, twenty-seven. A girl for whom marriage had been difficult. Here he was, the glaring proof thereof. When the ceremony began, he realized that he didn't know the name of his wife-to-be. He asked her. She smiled beneath her veil and said: "Maria." The orthodox priest handed over a ring, asked them if they were ready to be joined in the sacred ties of holy matrimony—both answered in a clear voice, on which bobbed an uncertain airiness and a dubious mirth, that they were—then, joining their hands with the white cloth that in Serbia is called the *prevez*, blessed them. The banquet that Miloš had been waiting for followed. It took place, traditionally, in the groom's house, but as that house no longer had a groom, and Miloš no house, the villagers made at a brisk pace for the house of the father of the bride, where a long table had been hastily set during the ceremony. The two serving girls who had washed Miloš finished laying the silverware beside the plates. The men sat at one end of the table and the women at the other. Maria remained standing, as per tradition, to one side. Miloš gestured at her to come and sit with him. She looked at her father, who shook his head. Miloš rose, took her hand, and forced the young woman down beside him. The Rumelians grumbled, but as this unheard-of event—a wife beside her husband during their wedding dinner—coincided with the arrival of the first course and above all with the jugs of wine and *rakia*, their reaction went no further. Maria's father whispered in Miloš' ear: "That isn't done." The Serb replied: "Marrying a girl you don't know without knowing why and swearing to her father you'll disappear the next day, that's done?" The Greek was silent for a moment, then raised his glass to Miloš' health. The villagers followed suit. There were songs and speeches. After the hors d'oeuvres, grilled lamb was served. Miloš drank and ate abundantly. It seemed to him he had not eaten thus for five years, eight months, and thirteen days. He used only his right hand, and his wife used only her left, for his left and her right remained joined beneath the table, one in the other's.

The Serb related several battles from the war for independence. The Rumelians listened, gaping. They had before them a hero of their country's liberation, and a foreigner besides. Was this why they let him ride roughshod over their customs, even when he refused Maria's godfather the privilege of accompanying the young couple to their room? When Maria squeezed his hand several times under the table, he understood that if he drank any more it would be too much. He kissed his wife on the mouth. It was their first kiss. He smelled garlic, wine, onions, hot pepper, and milk. Maria gave gifts out to the guests. Shirts for the men, handkerchiefs and napkins for the women. The newlyweds mounted the stairs to a room prepared for their intentions. Miloš had not slept in clean sheets for several months; he wondered if he would not fall sound asleep as soon as he lay down upon them. Eleven o'clock. The guests made a ruckus with the plates, knives, forks, and glasses to chase demons away. Miloš and Maria undressed and climbed in bed. The Serb was not surprised to find the Greek no longer a virgin. He had expected something of the sort. The next morning, Miloš opened his wrist with his knife and pressed his arm to the sheets. When the diameter of the stain satisfied Maria, he withdrew his arm and she made him a dressing discreet enough that no villager would see it beneath his shirt. They dressed at the same time, on opposite sides of the bed, without looking at each other. Maria's godfather had fallen asleep behind the door. He leapt up, ran into the room, saw the bloodstain, dashed down to the courtyard, and fired his gun into the air, waking the last guests dozing off before their cake.

When all the guests had gone home, Miloš kissed Maria on both cheeks and took the path to the sea, where he thought to sail that very night, or the morning after, for Montenegro. From there, Belgrade. He asked Maria if she wanted to explain what had happened. She said that she was carrying her father's child. Her fiancé had found out and had had to be replaced. Then she turned her back on Miloš—that magnificent back on which he'd fallen asleep, then woken, then fallen asleep again so many times during the night.

My Grandfather

Peter Huchel | Translated by Ken Fontenot from German (Germany)

The most powerful way to say a thing in German is not always the most powerful way to say it in English. Adjustments must be made, the text finely tuned. So should we alter the original text even slightly in our target text? Of course, if it calls for that. Equivalencies often don't suffice. Translating Huchel poses no real problem for the alert translator. Some of his poems come across better than others. One of them, "My Grandfather," came to me in one sitting of about an hour. In a prose piece in his *Collected Works*, Huchel talks about how, as a ten year old in 1913, his first reading experiences began among his grandfather's forestry and hunting archives, for his books were not aimed at the usual ten year old's inter-

ests: Sinbad the Sailor or Robinson Crusoe, for example. Raised by his strict Prussian grandfather, he feared the ruler used for whippings. From the elder Huchel's books, Peter read about the cannibalism of Afghan hounds, the strange memory of a pointer, and about how to poison wolves with crow's eyes, to mention just a few topics. Nature, the open air, with all its manifestations, made a great impression on the young Huchel, while his grandfather's books were teaching tools for German and French foresters, hunters, and sportsmen. And Huchel lived among men who knew how to survive the extreme cold of East Prussian winters.

Originally an East German poet from the Brandenburg area, Peter Huchel (born in 1903) was eventually asked to step down from his duties as editor of the highly praised literary journal, *Sinn und Form*, which he headed up from 1949 to 1962, when party requirements forced him to compromise his artistic integrity. He went into an imposed isolation for eight years in the East, but was granted permission to settle in West Germany in 1971. Unfortunately he didn't live to see the uprising that united the two Germanys in late 1989. He died in 1981, having witnessed the repeated existential and political catastrophes of his torn country.

Original Text: Peter Huchel, "Mein Grossvater" from *Gesammelte Werke, Band I, Die Gedichte* (1984). Reprinted with friendly permission of Suhrkamp Verlag Frankfurt am Main.

Mein Grossvater

Tellereisen legen,
das Aufspüren des Marders bei frischem Schnee,
das Stellen von Reusen im Mittelgraben,
das war sein Metier.

Für die Auerhahnjagd
die curische Büchse.
Sie schoß ein Blei,
das nicht stärker als ein Kirschkern war.

Er pirschte mit dem Jagdhund voraus,
ich verkroch mich in den blakenden Abend,
sah über der verschneiten Eiche
am Himmel den Hirsch verbluten.

My Grandfather

Laying steel traps.
Tracking down martens in fresh snow.
Putting fish traps in the middle ditch.
That was his trade.

For his grouse hunts
a Courland gun.
Its lead shot was
no more powerful than a cherry pit.

With his hunting dog he stalked ahead.
In the smoky evening I crawled into hiding,
saw, above the snow-covered oak,
a deer bleeding to death in the sky.

Was wär, wenn ich fortliefe
und ließe ihn mit seinen Netzen,
Remisen und Fallen allein?
Ich ging nicht über die sieben Seen.

In strengen Wintern saßen
die Rebhühner nah bei den Scheunen.
Mit rauher Zunge leckte der Mond
das klamme Fell der Katze.

Scharf und brandig stand die Luft
dort über dem Schnee.
Der Alte kam hinter der Miete hervor
und trug die Flinte ins Haus zurück.

Prophetisch begann die Nacht,
messianisch die erste Stunde.
Er kramte im Bücherkasten und las
die »Volksschriften zur Umwälzung der Geister«.

What if I ran away
and left him alone with his nets,
his game shelters, his traps?
I didn't sail the seven seas.

In harsh winters the partridges
perched close to the barns.
With its rough tongue the moon
licked at the cat's clammy fur.

There over the snow the air
was keen and smelled of burning.
The old man emerged from behind the potato pit
and carried his gun back into the house.

The night began prophetically;
its first hour was Messianic.
He rummaged around in the bookcase and read
the *Popular Works Toward a Spiritual Upheaval.*

Er drehte am Messingring der Lampe.
Die Sonne glomm auf,
der Eichelhäher schrie
und flog in den kalten märkischen Morgen.

He turned the lamp's brass ring.
The sun glimmered.
The jay cried out and flew
into the cold morning of Brandenburg.

Two Poems from *Jaula*

Astrid Cabral | Translated by Alexis Levitin from Portuguese (Brazil)

Astrid Cabral was born in Manaus, in the heart of the Amazon. Though she lived in a major capital with an opera house, nature was intensely present throughout her childhood. Having left her hometown at the age of eighteen, she has lived in Brasilia, Rio de Janeiro, Chicago, Beirut, and London, but the creatures of her early memories, along with their often exotic Amazonian names, have accompanied her wherever she has gone. They include bats rustling in the eaves, frogs in ditches, wasps, fireflies, lizards, geckos, pet parrots, land turtles, freshwater turtles, roosters, hens, dogs, cats, goats, and, just beyond the yard, boa constrictors. In shallow branches of the nearby river, she would gather minnows and tadpoles in her hands, while further out the pink back of the mysterious river dolphin would smoothly arch its way through the dark waters. This is the world she came from, and it remains deeply rooted in her blood and in her dreams.

I have translated many of Astrid Cabral's poems, but the translation that first caught her eye was "White Whale." The poet is, of course, deeply attached to the natural world and its creatures, but she is also highly attentive to language and the nuances inherent in the sounds of words. So she was pleased by my evident effort to reflect her sound-play in this long and amusing exercise. The first two lines, for example, could have simply been "Through wet blue / the white whale dances," but the assonance of "úmido azul" and the playful consonantal and assonantal echoes in "baleia albina baila" would have been utterly lost. Instead, my version provides a plethora of assonance and alliteration, too much, one might fear, if the poem were not so buoyantly droll: "Through humid hued blue / the white whale weaves." Later on, three verbs dance assonantly together, "nadam dançam / se lançam," while, in English, alliteration, as is often the case, must compensate for the lost assonance, "weave wave / wander" (note how the alliterative attraction has seduced me into the repetition of the verb from line two, "weave"). One last example of Astrid Cabral's playfulness and my attempt to be worthy of it: "pelos pastos salgados / da algas e sargaços." The intermingling of alliterative and assonantal effect is rather dazzling and my effort falls short, but here it is: "through salty pastures / of branching thallus and Sargasso." I stuck with the relatively unfamiliar botanical term "thallus" for the sake of the complex resonances between the "th" and two "s" sounds, surrounding the assonance, though "seaweed" would have alliterated with Sargasso. These are the choices we make and rarely is there certainty. But that is the challenge and the pleasure of the craft.

Original Text: Astrid Cabral, "Adeus" and "Baleia albina" from *Jaula*. Rio de Janeiro: Editora de Palavra, 2006.

Adeus

De manhãzinha qualquer
latido me apunhalava.
Era nosso brinquedo favorito
e foi enterrado no jardim
com o ritual de praxe:
Velas e rezas, choro e flor.
Só não teve missa que
nesse tempo era em latim.
Quando o capim cresceu
regado pelas chuvas
passávamos as mãos nele
dizendo: o pêlo mudou de cor.

Farewell

Early in the morning any
bark would stab me like a dagger.
He had been our favorite playmate
and was buried in the garden
with all the customary rites:
candles and prayers, tears and flowers.
Mass alone was missing since
back then it was in Latin.
When the grass grew thick
watered by the rains
we would stroke it with our hands
and say: his fur has changed its color.

Baleia albina

Pelo úmido azul
      a baleia albina baila
e assombra
      a sala em penumbra
barbatanas rêmiges
      a massagear
volumosa massa d'água
      o trêmulo transparente
      corpo marinho…
Marítima mamífera
      a espraiar
      a cútis de elanca
Enquanto as gordas vastas ancas
      nadam   dançam
       se lançam

White Whale

Through humid hued blue
          the white whale weaves
a startling dance for
          the darkened room
fins fanning
          massaging
vast masses of water
          transparent trembling
          body of the sea…
Marine mammal
          stretching out
          its elastic skin
While its vast and massive hips
          weave   wave
          wander

pelos pastos salgados
          de algas e sargaços...
Será menina
          a baleia albina?
Será adulta
          a náufraga lua animal?
Ou centenária
          a submarina cetácea nau?
Senhora dona do aquático sítio
          supondo-se
          solitária soberana
desfila   tranqüila na líquida passarela
          e revela
          coreografia de estrela
          e solfeja
cantiga de amor aquiantiga
          e corteja
sem saber-se a prima-dona
          de um mega espetáculo
sem pressentir
          a intimidade exposta

through salty pastures
       of branching thallus and sargasso...
Could it be a child,
       the white white whale?
Could it be an adult
       shipwrecked animal moon?
Or centenarian
       a submarine cetacean ship?
Lady mistress of that aquatic place
       imagining herself
       solitary sovereign
she parades   tranquil on the liquid runway
       and reveals
       the choreography of a star
       and sings solfeggios
 of old love songs ancient of ancients
       and flirts
without knowing herself the prima donna
       of a mega-spectacular
without foreseeing
       that intimacy exposed

à ribalta de mil olhos
         pelo globo em volta…
Como o mar tão vasto
         cabe entre sofás?
Como nos toca o mar
         se a pele não nos molha?
À noite os gatos são pardos
À noite somos jonas e pinóquios
         acomodados na barriga da sala
         essa estranha baleia
cujas   paredes   entranhas
         o oceano invade
         e lambe até tarde…
Somos então outra casta de peixes
         pescados nas malhas
         de electrônica rede.

by the footlights of a thousand eyes
           throughout the whole surrounding globe…
How can the sea so vast
           fit between sofas?
How can the sea touch us
           if it doesn't wet our skin?
At night all cats are black
At night we are all Jonas and Pinocchios
           housed in the belly of the room
           that strange whale
whose   walls   bowels
           the ocean invades
           and laps till it grows late…
And so we are another sort of fish
           caught in the meshes
           of an electronic web.

Our Years of Beauty

Bogdan Suceavă | Translated by Sean Cotter from Romanian (Romania)

Two main problems faced me in translating this story; one I resolved through craft, the other through prayer. The story depends on an assumed attitude toward the Romanian Communist setting. A beauty queen, some beer, a stunt, and even an ending ex machina do not make much of a story, unless we can feel the irritation of the late 1980s Communist details: shabby housing, ridiculous medical care, propagandistic broadcasting. Communism strives to thwart the simple act of a beach vacation. But the English-language reader might not recognize the markers of this setting, might not feel the burden signaled in cheap cigarettes or a choral music festival. To help the reader understand the story's attitude toward Communism, I looked for places to amplify the narrator's anger by letting obscenity break his narration. In Romanian, he says his friend got "a serious beating" from his father; in English, the father "beats the shit out of him." His friend's anatomy is not "mixed up" but "ass-backwards," and rather than being angered by the choral music, the narrator says it "pissed me off." The danger of these translation choices is that they might throw off the balance of period detail and teenage fun. This problem, however, is the same as that which the characters themselves face.

The second problem also concerned balance: the description of the friend's anatomy borders on magical realism: a heart enveloped in a web of arteries? That note was out of place in an otherwise realistic story. But during a recent sermon, my priest told the story of his father, who was admitted for emergency open heart surgery when tests had revealed 100% blockage of his arteries. Only on cracking open his chest did the surgeon see that the man's arteries had sprouted hundreds of capillaries to circumvent the blockage. The surgeon sewed up the man's perfectly functioning heart without making any alteration. When I translated the description of the heart, I also made no alteration.

Original text: Bogdan Suceavă, "Anii noştri cei mai frumoşi" from *Imperiul generalilor tărzii şi alte istorii*. Cluj-Napoca: Editura Dacia, 2002.

Anii noştri cei mai frumoşi

Stăteam pe prosop, ne prăjeam la soare în mijlocul mulţimii şi ascultam *Radiovacanţa* Costineşti. Pe vremea aceea, cel mai de preţ lucru care venea din difuzoarele de pe plajă era tonul: semăna atât de mult cu *Europa Liberă* încât nu ne mai trebuia nimic. Era altceva decât festivalul de muzică corală contemporană transmis pe programul 1. Berea se încălzise, iar ţigara ne ardea pe gât. Simţeam sticla caldă în mână şi urmăream pe cer un nor în formă de tub. Îngropasem radioul în nisip.

Prietenul meu mă trezise dis-de-dimineaţă, în camera noastră de la căsuţe, ca să mă aducă aici, pe plajă, unde un milion de concursuri se desfăşurau în faţa celei mai pestriţe lumi care se adunase vreodată. Îşi pierduse minţile ieri noapte din pricina reginei frumuseţii. Parcă îl lovise cineva în cap şi-l schimbase cu totul. „Repede!", făcea trăgând de mine în zori, „o să înceapă." Prea multă bere în seara de dinainte: eram sfârşit din prima clipă a zilei.

Acum ne uitam către terasă. El se uita mult mai atent, eu zăceam la soare, fără să ascult nimic, plutind într-o somnolenţă vărateacă. Eram pierduţi între cei o mie privind cu gura căscată la noua regină a frumuseţii, proaspăt încununată ieri seară, către miezul nopţii. Părea înaltă, de acolo de unde o priveam noi, cu nasul ei în vânt şi aerul ei orgolios, mai potrivit starletelor din anii '50 decât vedetelor de mucava ale anilor noştri. Prea multă bere în cursul dimineţii, mă purtase năluca dincolo de gânduri, dincolo de durere. Prin mine treceau sunetele, trecea soarele. Deschideam ochii numai din când în când.

Pe vremea aceea Serbările Mării însemnau ceva. Nu era carnavalul de la Rio, îţi mai aduci aminte...

Our Years of Beauty

We lay on our towels, a host of young bodies baking in the sun and listening to Radio Vacation Costineşti. In those years, the best thing coming from the loudspeakers was the announcer's voice, the pace, the jokes. It was like Radio Free Europe for us, much better than the choral music festival on Romania One. The beers got warm, the cigarettes burned our throats. I held a solar-heated bottle in my hand and watched a cloud shaped like a tube. I buried the radio in the sand.

My friend had gotten me up early in the morning and dragged me from our tiny, cinder-block room down to the beach, where a thousand different contests were being held in front of the most stone-faced audience ever assembled. He had fallen for that year's beauty queen, when she was crowned at midnight the night before. It was like he'd been smacked on the head; he was a man

transformed. "Come on!" he said, at dawn, pulling on my arm, "it's starting." Too much beer the night before. I woke up already a wreck.

We looked over at the bar. His eyes were searching for something, I was just squinting in the sun, deaf to the world, floating in a summertime somnolence. I was lost in the crowd gathered to gape at the new Miss Costineşti. She seemed tall, from where we were. She held her nose in the air, proudly, more like a 1950's starlet than one of our cardboard celebrities. My spirit floated beyond thought, on the river of beer I was drinking to dull my pain. Sounds passed through me, sunlight passed through me. My eyes squinted and closed in alternation.

Back then, the Seaside Festivals were something. Not Carnival in Rio, sure, but when the city of Neptun awoke at dawn and drew back the smoke curtains thrown over it by the sea, we all went crazy. We ran to the beach from the vacation houses, where the people who had a bed to themselves were lucky, or lonely, or us. Then, there was an invasion from the lake on the other side of the main road. A flotilla of marvelous commandos and vestal virgins held symbols of the sea. We scrambled for copies of *Sequence*, a rag printed in Constanța by the Communist Youth Union and the staff of a local paper, full of double entendres for us to catch, with our beardless wits and jejune consciences. The air was full of winking jokes, making us feel smarter than we were and strong enough for anything.

Beer was the only thing to drink, those days, in Costinești, including the autochthonous bitter. That was only good cold, but now nothing was cold on Planet Earth. We clinked our bottles and left them to heat up in the sun: we could not get another mouthful down. The beauty queen this year was better looking than last year's, who I remembered very well. My friend might have been right, but still, he was not acting rationally. It was like he was possessed.

Suddenly, my friend got off his towel, jumped out of the crowd with his hand in the air. "Me! Me!" He ran through the wasteland of tightly packed bodies and headed for the bar. "Come on!" I went after him, without knowing where I was going. "What's with you?" I said, "Where are we going?"

"To stand on our heads."

I thought of gym class, the eleventh grade. The teacher had us perform a series of gymnastic maneuvers, culminating in a headstand. I had struggled mightily. My greatest achievement of the spring was to stand, just once, on my head. I looked awful on a normal day. My enormous head was set on a skinny neck, supported by a perfectly round torso that reached the ground by way of two thin legs. When I lifted them up in front of the class, my throat shook like it would snap in two. But I accomplished my mission. I had been practicing for two months on whatever pillows, mattresses, and blankets I could find. Around the same time, all of our bedding had caught on fire, when an improvised space heater made one of the outlets burst into flames. I practiced at home on stacks of burnt-smelling blankets, the same ones my father pulled over himself at night.

I followed my friend toward the bar, where one of the organizers stopped us. "I'm here for the headstand contest," my friend said and looked up at the guy who looked down on us. "And him, what's he doing here?" said the guy. "What if everyone came running into the bar with their beers?"

"But I need him to hold my things."

"Okay, but don't let anyone see." The guy gave me a place to stand, some distance from the contest. The truth was, my friend didn't have any things for me to hold. He was naked, except for his suit, and he wasn't carrying anything but a beach towel.

Only then did I realize this wasn't a joke. A dizziness washed over me. I looked at the sea in its afternoon colors (the water is deep along the beach, you remember, the Costineşti beach, torn from paradise), and the thousands of longhaired heads heroically braving the afternoon sun, many of whom were looking back at the bar, waiting for the performance.

My friend went to the emcee, who introduced him with a dramatic gesture. That's when I heard the rules for the first time. Whoever stood on his head for fifteen minutes would get to go for a long paddleboat ride, accompanied by Miss Costineşti. It was glory itself.

We should have known something was up: it was the only time one person volunteered for a contest. Usually there were dozens.

Suddenly I realized, with utter clarity, my friend was in real danger. The previous spring, he had been x-rayed from head to toe and ended up seeing specialists in Bucharest after some routine follow-ups for a hormone imbalance revealed that his entire body was put together ass-backwards. His liver was on the left, he had three kidneys, one jammed in sideways, and his appendix was the size of a lung. Furthermore, one of his arteries had split into a hundred tiny tubes, wrapped around his heart like a spider web.

He carefully folded his flimsy beach towel into a yellow square and put it down, not two steps from the throne of the beauty queen. He laid on the tiles before her. For a moment he was still, in the absolute silence of the crowd, then he pushed his legs into the air and became unshakeable again. Shouts and applause erupted from the beach. Thousands of eyes turned to the upside-down arc of his shoulders and admired his abdomen, flat with effort. A thin body drawn toward the sky.

She sat on a chair showered in wilting lilies, protected by a rainbow-colored umbrella. She wore a blue swimsuit, one-piece, and a small crown in her hair. Up close, like this, she was astonishingly beautiful.

Just after the doctors discovered his bizarre anatomy, my friend's dad had beat the shit out of him for doing chemistry experiments in the bathtub. My friend had investigated the combination of solder, lime, pumice stone, margarine, and soda water. For a while he tried to lie about it, but even I wasn't sure: was he really planning on drinking that concoction? Apparently, once he found out his anatomy was so different, he became curious to see if he had special powers. So he drank a variety of things. He could already drink twice as much beer as me; he was smart as a whip; he was an amazing soccer player who could dribble, run, and dance with the ball and would do a bicycle kick over cement without holding back; and he knew our town like the back of his hand. He was unstoppable, and every day he felt he had to prove himself all over again. He was different, this he knew for sure.

After a full minute, he turned red from foot to head. I could see his feet were shaking. The crowd could see his profile, because he had been sure to face the beauty queen, who watched him from her chair, two steps away. It occurred to me that he might be doing this just to look at her from an unusual angle.

This all happened the same summer that they found, in a ditch by the old fortress wall, a beautiful blond girl's dead body. They still haven't found out who killed her. Not even a rumor. This summer was different, one we will remember in every detail. For example, there was one night when I told my friend how Vlad Țepeș had screwed Târgoviște when he moved Romania's capital to Bucharest. Țepeș abandoned us, left us in a provincial sleep from which we never awakened. My friend agreed:

it was clear that one day the entire town would bore itself to death.

As he stood on his head in front of a thousand people, two steps from the beauty queen, I saw what everyone could see, the growing protuberance of his swimsuit. He looked at the queen and died a little inside. His trembling became more intense and the veins on his throat thickened. His wrists shook against the floor of the bar. His eyes rolled back into his head.

The emcee was busy announcing the contest for post-sitting. The contestants, tied together two by two, had to stand on narrow platforms, built like miniature gallows ten feet above the beach. Dozens of volunteers lined up, and the crowd's attention shifted elsewhere.

I could see how the beauty queen stared at my friend. As his swimsuit expanded enough to hold the moon in the mists of late September, so her pride, two steps away, began to melt. In the end, the beauty queen turned back into a woman and asked, "Do you feel alright? Do you need anything?" loud enough for me to hear, even where I was.

It was a mistake. My friend had been trying to forget her, to close his eyes and get a hold of his dizziness. But now she wouldn't leave him alone. "Ggggg," was all he could manage, as a sign that he wanted nothing.

On the beach, nutty couples were climbing onto the platforms. A photographer for *The Sequence* began to immortalize the moment. Well, he had a newspaper badge on. He might have been doing it for fun.

Eight minutes passed. I knew my friend could never last so long. I don't think he had ever tried to stand on his head before. There are people who practice headstands. This was not our case. We had never heard of yoga, we had lives to live, bands like *Iris* and *Compact* to listen to, films to see, dancing to do. Our minds were elsewhere. As many beers as we had had, I'm surprised we still knew our own names.

Then my friend's suit calmed down, and his face turned purple. He shook like a cat in a tree. Radio Vacation Costineşti played a song we liked: "Imagine," by John Lennon.

Before we came to the beach, in May sometime, my

friend had started to go on walks around town with a girl from his class. That was the first time he'd ever tried to impress someone with his unusual anatomy. He told me she was not at all enchanted by his three kidneys. She had made up some excuse and left him, in the middle of his confession, in the middle of the street. Utterly miserable, he had gone home and called me.

I looked at the clock. He only had to last two more minutes. "Imagine all the people," sang John Lennon.

It happened at fourteen minutes and twenty seconds. He hit the cement like a bag of potatoes, with a loud smack that went through the air, ran over the shoals to the shipwreck, beyond the nude beach, toward the village and German bunkers, where the shore was littered with sea-lion carcasses.

He lay on his stomach, coughing like a dog. He rubbed the elbow where he had landed on the cement. John Lennon had said all he had to say. The fall posed a problem for the contest organizers, since they hadn't thought of a consolation prize.

Then the beauty queen regained the air of glory which had won over the virgins of the midnight past. She rose from her throne, knelt down by my friend and embraced him. I thought she was trying to help him stand up, but no, she was saying something. Her hair fell onto his shoulders.

Then the emcee moved toward them and said, "A hand for our contestant from Târgoviște, who came so close to winning…" and some other meaningless things.

She walked away from my friend. He gathered himself up and we left the bar, passing well under the shoulders of the enormous man. We sat at a table in front of the locked-up donut stand and looked at each other. We didn't say a word. The metal chair burned my thighs, and I couldn't be bothered to move. The sound of the sea was drowned out by the wheezing recorded music, something by Modern Talking. Usually, this band would get a rise out of my friend. It wasn't even funny now. All the joy of vacation was destroyed.

We felt frustrated, thrown onto the edge of a world that was happy without us of obscure signs and wonders. We felt alone.

Suddenly, the bombastic voice of the emcee announced the next event of the Seaside Festival: "We now present to you a team of medical specialists from the University Hospital in Cluj. These doctors will judge the next contest, held under the aegis of the Ministry of Health and the Association of Communist Students. To the right of the bar, they have set up a mobile x-ray machine, because our next contest is for—bizarrest anatomy! The rules are simple: the most unusual x-ray wins the prize. Contestants please come to the bar. The winner receives a ride on the sea with the beauty queen, in a paddleboat covered with flowers…."

My friend turned toward me with feverish eyes. He said, as though in a dream, "I'm going to knock them dead. If three kidneys don't win, what can?" He winked at me quickly and smiled confusedly, then he threw me his towel and ran toward the bar. That's when I remembered the radio I had buried in the sand two hours earlier, when the choral festival had pissed me off.

The Old English *Rune Poem*

Anonymous | Translated by John Estes from Old English (England, 10th century)

This translation of the *Rune Poem* (about a quarter of which appears here) was motivated, as most are, by a sense that existing versions were not adequately reproducing or interpreting the text in some essential way. I found them either too literal to offer the pleasures of poetry or too contemporary to convey the verbal density and dexterity of the Old English. Beyond that, there is an historical inheritance from earlier Germanic and Scandinavian versions that even to an Anglo-Saxon must have made it sound at least slightly foreign. Because this poem was composed during the Anglo-Saxon transition from orality to literacy, I've tried to activate here what I see in the original: a drama where the poet, with some ironic distance, is aiding readers to navigate this noetic strait within the form of the abcedarium and the trope of the *futhorc* runes. My guiding conjecture is that the poet had a sense, however nascent, of the changes this technology promised to an oral culture ill-equipped for it beyond the fatalistic brace of catastrophe. In most of the *Rune Poem*, the poet deals with matters squarely external—celebrating collective life, scenes of the natural world, suggesting readers recall and take comfort in the orders of family and town against the threat of elements and enemies. But a few of the runes focus upon individual finitude and are painfully cognizant of our individual separateness and the loneliness, despite whatever eternal hope, of death. The *Rune Poem*, like other wisdom literatures, seeks to provide strategies, even exercise, in understanding and addressing the demands of life and assumes—an assumption of literate cultures—that the world can in some way be read and known. In this confluence of familiarity and strangeness lies its georgic practicality, and my primary effort has been to charge the *Rune Poem*—too often treated as historical artifact—with the kind of vitality it would have possessed to tenth-century auditors and readers, restoring to (or preserving in) the English playful ambiguities present in the extant original. I have sought, with hopes not to strain the modern ear, to conjure a bit of the old *geglengan* and *wel geworht*, the ornamented and well-wrought qualities Bede identified as the style and aura of Old English poetry.

The Old English *Rune Poem*

ᚹ *wyn*

ne brūceþ   ðe can wēana lȳt
sāres and sorge,   and him sylfa hæfþ
blǣd and blysse   and ēac byrga geniht.

Enjoyment

Delight strives to avoid misfortune's favor
and refuses to graze on sorrow; it owes
its riches to friends, custom and a strong gate.

ᚻ *hægl*

byþ hwītust corna;   hwyrft hit of heofones lyfte,
wealcaþ hit windes scūra;   weorþeþ hit tō wætere
      syððan.

Hail

The whitest grain, heaven's tempests throw it
      swirling down;
winds with violent broadcast hurl it, then later harvest
      rills of water.

īs

byþ ofereald,   ungemetum slidor,
glisnaþ glæshlūttur   gimmum gelīcust,
flōr forste geworuht,   fæger ansȳne.

gēr

byþ gumena hiht,   ðonne God lǣteþ,
hālig heofones cyning,   hrūsan syllan
beorhte blēda   beornum ond ðearfum.

Ice

Colder than cold, slippery without dimension;
crystalline sun, gem of glistening clarity;
it grounds the burst font of beautiful springs.

Summer

The year ripens to joy when, God willing it,
a hale earth holds heaven to its king's pledge
and reaps a bright repast for chief and beggar.

↑ *tīr*

biþ tācna sum;   healdeð trȳwa wel
wiþ æþelingas;   ā biþ on færylde
ofer nihta genipu;   næfre swīceþ.

ᛗ *eh*

byþ for eorlum   æþelinga wyn,
hors hōfum wlanc,   ðær him hæleþ ymb,
welege on wicgum,   wrixlaþ sprǣce;
and biþ unstyllum   ǣfre frōfur.

Polestar

Sky-watcher's lonely waymark; oath-guard
and prince's tutor; journey-friend and door
to plagues of murk and night; ever faithful.

Steed

The well-born stride their mounts for weight
and sway, thrilled by a horse's proud hoofbeats;
fortuned soldiers brawl for their fetch's war-like
virtue; swagger quenches the drought of peace.

ᛚ *lagu*

byþ lēodum   langsum geþūht,
gif hi sculun nēþun   on nacan tealtum,
and hī sæȳþa   swȳþe brēgaþ,
and se brimhengest   bridles ne gȳmeð.

ᚪ *āc*

byþ on eorþan   elda bearnum
flǣsces fodor;   fereþ gelōme
ofer ganotes bæþ;   —garsecg fandaþ
hwæþer āc hæbbe   æþele trēowe.

Ocean

Lacking metes and bounds, the open-water seems
two-faced and brazen to seamen who reckon
with it; storm-swells tilt their hapless ships, scares
them stiff when the wave-horse's reins go slack.

Oak

Its fruit the fodder that feeds the creatures cut
for meat, children's food; its body hewn to boards
travels the gannet's bath, a husk-guard—choppy seas
will judge whether the noble oak has kept its troth.

The Snares of History

Georges Anglade | Translated by Josephine Berganza from French (Haiti)

The following text is a *lodyan*: an oral genre from Haiti that, according to the author Georges Anglade, is as inseparable from Haitian culture as Voodoo, Creole or Carnival. The *lodyan* distinguishes itself by its brevity; each word is considered for its ability to move the story towards its climax without delay. Sparring storytellers shoot off their *lodyans*, and as the stories rattle towards their punch line, the gathered audience delivers the verdict on their success or failure.

Georges Anglade, a professor of geography now living in Montreal, describes feeling a "fiction emergency" which compelled him to commit his *lodyans* to paper. He explores his personal experiences, which include being held political prisoner in 1974, and delves into Haiti's collective memory (and collective forgetfulness). A precarious view of Haiti emerges: marooned between the Africa it left behind and the America it has yet to reach. Anglade associates *lodyans* with freedom of speech, noting that Haiti's famous storytellers were the first to disappear during Duvalier's dictatorship. The generic form is only recently being revived, with Anglade himself leading the way.

It is not for nothing that storytellers "shoot off" *lodyans*—they deliver a powerful punch in relatively few words. The major difficulty in translation, therefore, was maintaining the level of impact that the texts generate.

In many ways, much of what one applies to traditional French translation had to be un-learned. Usually, Gallic verbosity is trimmed down in order to fit Anglo concision. But here, there is no excess. Double, and sometimes triple, entendres are seamlessly woven into the briefest of sentences.

I did not want to "choose" a reading of the texts. I felt that it was crucial to remember that this is an oral form: these stories are destined for an audience and they should, rightly, evoke different associations for different people. This means that some of the translated sentences are longer than in the original French, so in order to retain an effect of overall sharpness, I tried to take advantage of succinct English syntax at other points in the texts. I asked many people to read over my English translations. After all, a *lodyan* is a miniature piece of theatre and the texts' speed and delivery have to be considered. One question yet to be answered: would these English translations meet the approval of a Haitian audience finishing up Sunday afternoon at the beach?

Original text: Georges Anglade, "Les pièges de l'Histoire" from *Les Blancs de mémoire*. Montreal: Les Éditions du Boréal, 1999.

Les pièges de l'Histoire

Le pas était le même, quoique plus lent, la taille large n'avait pas trop épaissi, la silhouette trapue et surtout la *guayabera* blanche immaculée ne pouvaient tromper, même de dos. Il s'agissait bien du Cher Docteur, l'idéologue inspiré de la question de couleur qui avait contribué aux changements de 1946 et qui avait participé de près à la prise du pouvoir par François Duvalier en 1957. Il se promenait sur un large trottoir du Canapé-Vert, à Port-au-Prince, en route vers le marchand de crème glacée du coin, entouré de quatre petits-enfants, dont les deux plus jeunes qu'il tenait par la main. Tout ce petit monde piaillait et jacassait avec des accents du Québec, dans une confusion joyeuse entrecoupée de «Grand-père! Grand-père!».

Je réduisis machinalement ma foulée pour jouir de la scène, avant d'aller le saluer, pour qu'il prenne acte que je l'avais vu en pareille équipeé. La dernière fois, c'était il y a vingt-cinq ans, dans l'année terrible de 1965. Il était lors directeur des Archives et j'y sollicitais un relevé d'acte de naissance, démarche préalable à l'obtention d'un passeport pour un éventuel départ, si j'arrivais à passer au travers du filet aux mailles serrées, tendu par la dictature, contre l'émigration massive des jeunes professeurs vers l'Afrique. Il devait alors juste rentrer dans la cinquantaine, et sa feuille de route était impressionnante. Il m'avait longuement retenu dans son bureau, deux heures, ce qui était énorme, compte tenu de la moyenne journalière de trois heures de bureau de la fonction publique, pour nuancer sa caution à ce qui se passait et défendre son oeuvre d'historien et son combat politique. C'était un théoricien de choc du «noirisme» et un polémiste redoutable…

The Snares of History

His walk was the same, although perhaps a little slower than before, his large waist had not much thickened, but it was his stocky silhouette and above all his immaculate white *guyabera* which gave him away, even from behind. It was our Cher Docteur, an ideologist driven by the question of color who contributed to the changes of 1946 and who was close on hand during Francois Duvalier's takeover in 1957. He was walking down a wide street in Canapé-Vert, Port-au-Prince, on his way to the ice cream maker's on the corner, surrounded by four grandchildren, the youngest of which he held by the hand. The group of little people squealed and chattered with Canadian accents in a joyful confusion pierced by exclamations of "Grandfather! Grandfather!"

I slowed my pace mechanically in order to enjoy the scene before going to greet him, so that he would realize that I had seen him in his current company. The last time that I had seen him was twenty-five years ago, in that awful year: 1965. At the time he was head of Archives and I was asking for a copy of my birth certificate, a document that was required before requesting a passport. I planned to leave, if I could slip through the tight mesh of the dictator's net, held in place to try and curb the massive number of young professors emigrating to Africa. He must have been in his early fifties and his credentials were impressive. He kept me in his office a long while: two hours, which is an enormous length of time considering the average three-hour working day of civil servants, so that he could explain his sense of caution over current events, and defend his historical work and political fight. He was a radical thinker and a notorious polemicist who championed "blackism." Twenty years of research revealed that Haiti's national dynamic for the past two centuries essentially boiled down to a relentless struggle between Blacks and Mulattos, and was continuing still through a number of antagonistic battles between Old Independents and New Independents, Nationalists and Liberals, those caught up in collective *bovarysme* and those proud of indigenous culture, with slogans reminding us of the contradictory interests of the black majority and the mixed minority. He said that in his generation, the revolutionary position was pro-black. Thus he swore only by what was black, and yet dressed only in white.

There was no doubt in anyone's mind that the masses: homogeneously black, Creole-speaking, Voodoo-practicing, were frustrated by the independence that had been so hard to come by. The battle continued amongst those at the top, who for two centuries made up less than two percent of the population. With two hundred years of independence coming up in 2004, the priorities of the country still lie in working out mutually beneficial political and economic arrangements among the irremovable two percent of Bourgeoisie great and small, golden and downtrodden, and the different strata of all the middle classes. Two percent. After that come the people, the masses, misery. Even Apartheid in its day managed much better.

The two oldest children were becoming more and more excited and it was getting dangerous to let them run on their own with the sewer entrance yawning open at the foot of the neighborhood's mountain of household garbage. The Cher Docteur succeeded in forming a chain in which he was the central link, and the small hands, now better behaved, held one another two by two. Now safely tied together, the line of people affronted the last few meters' climb that led to the ice cream maker at the summit.

The question of color and her children came to the forefront of politics and Port-au-Prince affairs in 1946. The most significant investment conceded by the dominant factions was over the education of their heirs. These baby-boomers went to school together, studied the same subjects at universities all over the world, mixed a little when the time came for marriage and also took spouses and partners from the different places where they had spent their studious twenties.

The ice cream dribbled down tiny hands struggling to keep the cones upright. The grandfather's handkerchief went from one little face to the next, wiping here a little chocolate, there a little vanilla. The smallest girl's strawberry scoops had just fallen on the sidewalk, and she was trying in vain to rescue them, crying in a high-pitched voice. Her tears only stopped once she was presented with a brand new cone and two brand new scoops of strawberry ice cream. Perched on her grandfather's shoulder, she nonetheless continued to eye up the pink mound of ice cream that was slowly melting on the cement, warm from the end of the afternoon. The other three had already made themselves so thoroughly sticky that no intervention could save the shirts spotted with stains and streaked with the colors of double cones.

The generation who rushed onto the scene during the sixties added, to this question of the color of ancestors, social questions, gender questions and generational questions. And so the colorist grid lost its virulence. In the last ten years of the century, the final warning shots from the old school and its concluding rumblings of reticence at letting go, that we read about in *Le Nouvelliste*, no longer had the implications of times gone by.

He had managed to gather around him his small group in anticipation of the homeward leg of the expedition. It was at this moment that I chose to approach him. He recognized me straight away. Warmly. And with a hearty laugh that was worth a thousand words, he first introduced me to the two blond infants as his grandchildren, sons from the first marriage of his son-in-law from Saguenay, "You know, married to my daughter Ginette who teaches at Chicoutimi University," he said with a note of pride, and then to the two little Mulattos as the daughters of his youngest son, "You know, the great Sherbrooke doctor," adding with satisfaction that these days he holidayed with his family at Canapé-Vert.

During these introductions, the children were calling out "Grandfather! Grandfather!" to show him, laughing, his white *guayabera* daubed with strawberry pink.

A Cross of Candles

Carlos Ernesto García | Translated by Elizabeth Gamble Miller from Spanish (El Salvador)

Carlos Ernesto García is a poet of El Salvador, now a Spanish citizen, whose first volume of poetry was published in 1987. *Hasta la cólera se pudre* appeared in a second edition in 1994, the same year that the bilingual version, *Even Rage Will Rot*, was published by Cross-Cultural Communications, translation by Elizabeth Gamble Miller. Our collaboration has continued through three books of poetry; some twenty-five poems have been published in six literary journals, and his book of prose *Bajo la sombra de Sandino* is currently being translated. Interviews of eight ex-comandantes of the Nicaraguan Revolution were conducted by García in 2004 on the celebration of the twenty-fifth anniversary of the Sandinista victory. Carlos is also the author of *El sueño del dragón*, a novelized travel book of his trip to China. His poetry has been translated into Chinese and Italian, as well as English. García is a correspondent for the newspaper *Co Latino* in El Salvador, a journalist in Spain, and a cultural projects manager for C&Duke in Barcelona. His coordination of European journalists to document the 2001 earthquake devastation in El Salvador led to an anthology *El Salvador, entre la naturaleza y la mano del hombre*. He has been a guest of universities and institutions in Europe, Latin America, and the United States.

The poetry of García reflects his experiences of violence in his homeland, the pathos of losing his father and sister and his home to a brutal attack, and barely escaping with his own life. The loss of family is poignantly expressed, as in the lines of "They Are Like the Dew," from *Even Rage Will Rot.*

I have seen tears fall
upon silk of a pillow
others upon mud or grass
But there are those
that don't fall anywhere
as if held in reserve
for the rest of life.

The beauty and impact of these verses stem from the brevity of the poem, comprised of a single sentence. In three verses Carlos Ernesto García has portrayed all walks of life in their experience of pain with just the words "tears," "silk," "pillow," "mud," and "grass," and expressed the all-consuming grief that doesn't dissipate. "A Cross of Candles," from the unpublished manuscript "A Suitcase in the Attic," further illustrates Carlos Ernesto García's style. His poetry captures deep emotions through sharp images produced by simple vocabulary, action verbs, suppression of adjectives, and concrete nouns; the result is lyrical and rhythmic.

Original text: Carlos Ernesto García, "Una cruz de velas" from the unpublished manuscript *La maleta en el desván.*

Una cruz de velas

Sus pies desnudos
se balancean con la brisa de octubre
En la oscuridad un rumor de hombres
que apenas pueden distinguirse
por las bracitas de los cigarrillos.

Una anciana de rodillas
coloca varias velas sobre la tierra
formando con ellas una cruz
que iluminan el cuerpo del ahorcado.

Durante toda la mañana
lo había visto angustiado
buscando una vaca perdida.
Descalzo y sin camisa
Gritando hasta enronquecer.

A Cross of Candles

His naked feet
swing back and forth in the October breeze
In the darkness a muffled noise of men
you can barely distinguish
by their lighted cigarettes.

An old woman on her knees
arranges several candles on the ground
forming a cross with them
lighting the body of the one hanged.

All morning long
I had watched him
looking anxiously for a lost cow.
Barefoot and shirtless
Yelling until he was hoarse.

Lo conocía bien
Algunas madrugadas
él me brindaba en un huacal
la primera sangre de la res
que degollaba en la madrugada.
Para que creciera fuerte y recio
decía con su voz joven y alegre.
¡Tan fuerte!
¡Tan recio!
como el árbol de Amate
como la cuerda de maguey
que en su desesperación
encontró adecuados
para colgar su garganta

I knew him well
Some early mornings
he would offer me a gourd
of the first blood of the steer
he slaughtered that morning.
So I would grow big and strong
he would say with his happy, youthful voice.
So big!
So strong!
like the Amate tree
like the maguey rope
that in his despair
he found suitable
to tie around his throat

Making Things

Benilda Santos | Translated by José Edmundo Ocampo Reyes from Tagalog (Philippines)

Translating this poem was a process of *negotiation*: not only navigating the divide between Tagalog words and English approximations, but also seeking compromise between two radically different poetic traditions—the English-language tradition that eschews direct statement and hackneyed images like *moon* and *rain*, and the Tagalog tradition that accepts the presence of abstractions and everyday images. Because Santos values, in the words of Czeslaw Milosz, "plain speech in the mother tongue"—an impulse I tried to honor by choosing the simplest English approximations I could—seeking compromise was the more difficult challenge.

Take the title, for instance. *Paglikha* is made up of the prefix *pag-*, "the act of," and the root *likha*, "to make" or "to create." One way to translate the title into English would be as "Creation." To an English speaker, such a title would sound too blatant or cheesy, even though "Paglikha" is a perfectly fine title in Tagalog. The infinitive constructions "To Create" and "To Make" were similarly unacceptable.

I finally settled on the title "Making Things" after recognizing that the poem (from the Greek *póçma*, literally, "a made thing") is indeed an *ars poetica*:

And I will write:
I am a cloud, captive of light and darkness,

which until now has been no more than a veil to
    the moon
and until the end will be no more than a net for
    the rain.

Santos encounters the moon and rain, two of the most conventional poetic subjects, observing the binaries that most people would have likewise already noticed: rise and fall, roars and sobs. Yet despite the plethora of already-written poems about the moon and rain, she suggests, through the assertive "And I will write," that originality is still possible, and follows through with the striking image of a cloud "no more than a veil to the moon," "no more than a net for the rain." Paradoxically, it is in the poet's allowing herself to become a "captive of light and darkness," in her recognition of the futility of capturing the infinite, that she is able to present the quotidian in her own unique and mysterious way.

Original text: Benilda Santos, "Paglikha"
from *Pali-palitong Posporo: Mga Tula*.
Pasig City: Anvil Publishing, 1991.

Paglikha

Tuwing maghahanap ako ng tula
sa laktaw-laktaw na liwanag ng ulap sa gabi,
sa laganap na dilim ng ulap sa araw,
ang natatagpuan ko ay buwan at ulan.

Sa mukha ng buwan
nababasa ko ang paglusong at pag-ahon,
ang pagkukubli at paglalantad, at
ang himala ng pagiging malinis na ostiya ng langit
sa kabila ng maraming pilat.

Sa patak ng ulan
naririnig ko ang lagaslas at ragasa,
ang hikbi at hagulgol, at
ang himala ng pagiging dalisay na alak ng lupa
sa kabila ng alat at pait.

Making Things

Whenever I search for poems
in the evening clouds' intermittent light,
or in their spreading darkness by day,
I encounter the moon and rain.

In the moon's face
I can discern rise and fall,
disguise and unmasking,
and the miracle of becoming the sky's bright Host
despite so many scars.

In the rain
I hear roars and murmurs,
whimpers and sobs,
and the miracle of becoming earth's pure wine
despite the salt, the bitterness.

At isusulat ko:
Ako ang ulap na bilanggo ng liwanag at dilim,
na magpahanggang-ngayon lambong lamang ng buwan
at magpahanggang-wakas lambat lamang ng ulan.

And I will write:
I am a cloud, captive of light and darkness,
which until now has been no more than a veil to the moon
and until the end will be no more than a net for the rain.

Edgard's Lessons

Jean Sénac | Translated by Douglas Basford from French (Algeria)

Jean Sénac's position as a poet and radio broadcaster of European extraction who was promoting the work of native Algerian writers, and who was increasingly open about his homosexuality, led to tension with the government and even with the very writers he supported. "If singing my love is loving my country," Sénac begins one sonnet unapologetically, "I am a soldier who won't go back on what he said." He was murdered, by unknown hands, in the hovel in which he lived destitute for his last years.

I have been working on an early sequence, written almost two decades before his death, in the summer of 1954. *Edgard's Lessons* is a sequence of twenty-five in-tensely lyrical love poems for a young man about whom little is known except that he and Sénac had a troubled relationship that apparently ended just before Sénac fled to France on the eve of the Algerian Revolution. The sonnets, quatrains, and couplets attest to Sénac's European lineage, but his inflected syntax and diction spell out the tumult of homosexual eros and political commitment, both being—due to societal norms and governmental interference—latent and largely privately held, and later to become undeniably public, regardless of personal consequence. The preponderance of Sénac's poems published in English translation have been drawn from his later work of the 1960s and early 1970s, which was radical in style and content, having been influenced quite heavily by Char, Lorca, and Ginsberg. In order to understand this pivotal figure in Francophone writing across the transition from colonialism to post-colonialism, we must begin with the early poems of *Edgard's Lessons*.

Translating Sénac is much like translating Mallarmé: their sonnets move rapidly between images, frames of reference shifting, syntax a tangle at times. Whereas Mallarmé was preoccupied with language as a game, with the sonnet as a conventional yet arbitrary constraint, Sénac tended to see the sonnet as a near stand-in for his beloved, concluding one with a spill-over fifteenth line: "For you are / My disorder and my law." Thus, the challenge in translating him is maintaining the tension between order and chaos, eros and dejection. In this, one of the few non-sonnets in the sequence, his coupled and despairing questions and responses have the effect of casting Sénac as Echo calling after Edgard as Narcissus, who rather than being fixated on himself is happily socially adrift among the "others" that Sénac elsewhere "run[s] up against."

Original text: Jean Sénac, "Les leçons d'Edgard" from *Oeuvres Poétiques*. Arles: Actes Sud, 1999.

Les leçons d'Edgard

24

Ne dis rien. Où sommes-nous?
—Dans les plumes du hibou.

Ne ris pas. Où vent nos pas?
—Dans les marges du trépas.

Ne pleure pas. Où l'amour?
—Dans l'innocence du jour.

Où le pétale ? Où l'abeille?
—Sur la tartine qui veille.

Où le gain de nos élans?
—Dans le sourire et la dent.

Edgard's Lessons

24

Say nothing. Where are we now?
—Among the feathers of the owl.

Don't laugh. Where are our steps leading?
—Along the cusp of trespassing.

Don't cry. Can you say where love is?
—In the day's innocence.

Where is the petal? Where the bee?
—On the slice of bread that you see.

Where is our eagerness, its increase?
—In the smile and in the teeth.

Où la ruse du bon Dieu?
—Sous la crasse dans un creux.

Où ce que noun n'avons plus?
—Dans le sang comme un obus.

Où le soleil et la poutre?
—Dans le coeur qui s'élance outre.

Où l'honneur? Où l'or de l'homme?
—Dans ton froid comme une Somme.

Dans ton nom quand je te nomme.

Where the ruse of God's beneficence?
—Under the dirt in a trench.

Where is what we have no more of at all?
—In the blood like an artillery shell.

Where are the sun and its rays?
—In the heart which soars away.

Where is honor? Where man's gold?
—Like a Somme, in your coldness.

In your name when I name you.

Paradise

Claribel Alegría | Translated by Michael Henry Heim from Spanish (Nicaragua)

Claribel Alegría was born in 1924 in Estelí, Nicaragua, but from early childhood lived in the Santa Ana region of western El Salvador. She moved to the United States in 1943 and received a BA in Philosophy and Letters from George Washington University in 1948. During the 1960s she became involved in Central American politics, particularly with the Sandinista National Liberation Front (FSLN), whose grassroots movement in Nicaragua eventually overthrew the dictator Anastasio Somoza in 1979. In 1985 she returned to Nicaragua to aid in the country's reconstruction, and has resided there ever since.

Alegría's poetry and fiction have gained her wide recognition for her work on "historical testimony" in Latin America, and associate her with the Central American literary movement known as "la generación comprometida" (the committed generation). With her late husband, Darwin J. Flakoll, she collaborated on a number of testimonies, including *Death of Somoza*, *Tunnel to Canto Grande*, *The Sandinista Revolution*, and *They'll Never Take Me Alive*, as well as the novel *Ashes of Izalco*, about the 1932 *matanzas* (massacres) in El Salvador.

Her writing has won many awards, including Cuba's Casa de las Américas Prize (for *Sobrevivo* / I Survive) and the Independent Publisher Book Award for Poetry (for

Saudade/Sorrow). She has been honored by the Nicaraguan Academy of Language for her contribution to Central American culture and acknowledged by the Nicaraguan Writers Center for her valuable contribution to Nicaraguan Literature. In 2006 she became the nineteenth recipient of the prestigious Neustadt International Prize for Literature. Robert Con Davis-Undiano, executive director of Neustadt sponsor *World Literature Today*, called Alegría "one of the most courageous and revered Latin American writers of the past fifty years." Fellow Nicaraguan poet and Neustadt jury member Daisy Zamora said she nominated Alegría because "through her work, she verbalizes unresolved contradictions that plague Latin American societies, especially in Central America." Zamora said Alegría "unfailingly spoke up for liberty and justice, becoming the voice for the voiceless and dispossessed" and representing the struggle for liberation in Latin America.

Claribel Alegría's other works of poetry and fiction include *Soltando amarras/Casting Off* (2003), *Umbrales/Thresholds* (1996), *Fuga de Canto Grande/Fugues* (1992), *Luisa en el país de la realidad/Luisa in Realityland* (1987), and *La mujer del río/Woman of the River* (1989), as well as several children's books.

Original text: Claribel Alegría, "Paraíso."

On the original text of "Paraíso"

About twenty years ago I was asked to translate "Paraíso," the story that follows, for an anthology of contemporary erotic literature. Although Spanish is a language I do not usually work from, I eagerly undertook the project as a tribute to two undergraduate teachers I remember with special warmth: Clementine and Gregory Rabassa. (Clementine had just started teaching at Columbia at the time—it was the early sixties—and the two had not yet met. As I've told them since, I like to think that by moving from Clementine's Spanish language course to Greg's survey of Hispanic literature course I served as a kind of preliminary link.) Unfortunately the anthology came to naught, but through the years I dutifully converted the translation from WordStar to WordPerfect to Word. The original, however, having come to me in a typescript, disappeared in the interim, and search as I have among Alegría's collected stories I have been unable to locate it. I therefore present the translation not only as the tribute to two inspiring teachers but also as a possible addition to Alegría's oeuvre.

MICHAEL HENRY HEIM

Paradise

It was a Thursday evening. Débora sat in the driver's seat of her Ford Fiesta reading a mystery. She was waiting for her friends at the Motel Paraíso. Every so often she looked up and daydreamed.

Forty-five minutes, she said to herself, glancing at her pulsar watch. I hope they won't be much longer. But Claudia's only nineteen. I'm sure she's a virgin.

I was when I came here, she thought with a smile. Slightly older, though.

I wonder where they are now. Giuseppe's a real gentleman. He'd have ordered a bottle of whiskey, poured out a good swig for her, taken one himself, told her how pretty she is. Then he'd slip off her sandals and move round in back of her, unbutton her blouse with great tenderness and fondle her neck and breasts with his strong, stubby fingers. Slowly, masterfully.

Forty-five minutes is plenty of time. They'll be in bed by now—Giuseppe embracing her, inching his hand closer to her center, Claudia half-dead with fear, curiosity, desire.

He didn't believe me when I told him I was a virgin, silly man. Twenty-eight and a virgin! he said and burst out laughing. I thought I would die, but then he told me I smelled of sandalwood and my skin was as soft as jasmine petals.

She read three more pages, but couldn't concentrate. Claudia had no idea there'd been anything between Giuseppe and me; nobody knew. It was over before it began. I was glad to be rid of my virginity, I told my friends, but I never told them his name. They were so silly they refused to believe me. Why didn't I reveal his identity? Pride, most likely. Something told me it wouldn't last.

Next day he went back to Italy. He sent me a card from Milan saying I'd given him a fine time and he'd never forget me. "To the Virgin of Nicaragua," it began.

What made me bring them here? Why does Claudia go around with an older crowd? I was her best friend, after all, and Giuseppe was in his forties. Was the fore-play over yet?

"What's the matter with me?" she said aloud. "Why can't I concentrate?" she forced herself back to the mystery.

Two years ago, just after the Revolution, everything happened at once: instant marriages, instant divorces, instant adventures and love, love, love. Everyone was in love. Life pulsed through our veins.

Why didn't I follow suit? "Never trust a man," my mother used to say. "If he gets you into bed before you marry, he'll throw you out on your ear." Well, I've had my flings, but none has really scarred me. Not even Giuseppe, my first.

Watching them dance last night, I realized how they wanted each other, and I wasn't the only one. But with Clau-dia's mother there they couldn't just go off together. Claudia is a bit like me. Prettier, of course. Prettier and younger. If she's the butterfly, I'm the caterpillar. Or the mushroom perhaps. A hallucinogenic mushroom, a toadstool. And Giuseppe, what is he? A bird of passage. No cage for Giuseppe. Maybe Claudia's the one to tame him. She's so sweet, so affectionate.

"It's time for the Paraíso," I said, bringing their heads together, "for paradise." They both stared at me, amazed. "But on one condition: that you let me take you there."

"What are you talking about?" Claudia asked.

"I want to be the first to see you with burning cheeks."

Giuseppe gave me a telling look, but said nothing. I suddenly felt the world spin round, but here I am. Bringing Claudia to this place is a bit like bringing myself back.

She flipped through the pages of the mystery. I've completely lost interest. I'll just read the ending. I think I know how it turns out anyway.

They're in bed by now, skin to skin. Giuseppe is kissing her eyes, her mouth, her neck, trying to open her legs with his. I wonder what an orgasm is like. The only time I've come close is when I think of Papa in his coffin and see myself bending over his bandaged head, kissing his lips. "At last, Papa, at last."

Gilberto gave me the most pleasure, but of an innocent kind. He was a gentle soul. A bit awkward, a bit rushed, but he made me feel pretty and intelligent and understanding. Even though we were the same age, I felt like his mother. I don't think we went to bed more than ten times in the course of a year. Now I realize he was constantly looking for an excuse to get out of it and I never placed any demands on him. We never got to know each other, really. Then one day he was gone, without so much as a goodbye. He wrote to me from Rio saying he was gay. It didn't come as a surprise.

She put down the book, leaned back in her seat, and half-closed her eyes. I haven't known much suffering, actually, though my father's death—that did leave a scar. I was only nine at the time, but I knew no one would ever love me the way he did. I never saw him drunk. He would go off on binges for two weeks at a time, but he always came home with every hair in place and a present for me.

In some putrid cell, his skull smashed to bits. It was years before I learned the truth. Since then my life has been a faded tapestry with only the Revolution for highlights. My father let me down. Since his death my life has been one fiasco after the other.

It should be over by now. No, not yet. Claudia must be scared, poor thing. It hurts a little the first time. Never have I had such a rush of memories. The last time I felt good about myself was up in the mountains teaching peasants to read. A promising pupil, a brilliant student, then nothing. The best years of my life wasted in public relations, as an executive secretary—jobs with no meaning. Oh, I make a decent living and my friends look up to me—I'm always good for a laugh—but that wasn't what I wanted.

What *do* you want, Débora? I've always loved music, music and poetry. I'll never forget the fun I had with the oboe Papa gave me. If only I'd had a good teacher.

I've never felt a calling for anything. True, I wrote a few poems, but I preferred playing the pundit and criticizing others. I'm a deadly critic, people tell me. Where does it come from? Hostility, no doubt. I must have some existential flaw that keeps me from opening my eyes, arms, mouth, and heart wide enough to let life in.

The tears will be pouring down her cheeks now, and he's whispering sweet nothings in Italian. She'll probably fall in love with him. That's what I want, isn't it? What made me bring her here? It was bound to happen anyway, so why this compulsion to engineer it? Could it be revenge?

She sat up in the seat. No cars turning into the motel. I couldn't sleep last night. Something snapped. There's a battle going on inside me. I remember dreaming of a vast labyrinth. I've always had an affinity for the underground. I'm more mole than toadstool. What's left? I can't stand the thought of old age.

A long-buried thought sent a sudden charge through her body.

When Giuseppe and Claudia came back to the car, she seemed asleep, but Giuseppe heard the motor purring and saw the hose running through the window.

"She's dead."

Claudia let out a scream and flung herself, sobbing, on her friend's dead body. It was then and only then that she felt something akin to an orgasm.

Three Poems from *Mirrors of Dust*

Ibrahim Nasrallah | Translated by Omnia Amin and Rick London from Arabic (Palestine)

The Palestinian poet Ibrahim Nasrallah was born in 1954 in the Al Wehdat refugee camp in Jordan, where his parents had taken refuge in 1948. He lived in the camp for thirty-three years, attending the school sponsored by the United Nations Relief and Works Agency for Palestinian Refugees (UNRWA) and later studying at the UNRWA Teacher Training College in Amman. He is the author of fourteen books of poems and the recipient of numerous poetry awards and has also gained wide recognition as a novelist, photographer, and journalist.

In Nasrallah's poetry there is an unusual relationship of image to narrative. Returning figures, animate and inanimate, play host to the dramatic narratives they engender—by turns knowing and forlorn, often drawn out until the lyrical information accumulated begins to beckon to the reader like a parable.

These effects forge an intimacy between the reader and the poems. Often stately in tone, the work conveys a sense of distance and otherness and a loneliness felt in the interplay of solidarity and isolation, in the fragility of human connections, in the persistence of cruelty and injustice.

But if the universe Nasrallah conjures is often harsh, it is also a place of mystery and abundance where we sense the vast life the ordinary things around us are part of—a place where we see everyday things strangely and magically living out their lives on their own.

Omnia Amin and I began our translation partnership in May of 2003, a few weeks after the U.S. invasion of Iraq. I was in Amman, taking part in a cultural conference at Philadelphia University where Omnia was teaching. Although I don't know Arabic, I was invited to try my hand at brushing up some poems in translation. After I returned to San Francisco, Omnia and I began working together in earnest, with her overseeing my reworking of literal renderings of Arabic texts into English.

To give a sense of how things go on my end, I'd refer to an interview I heard with the actor Anthony Hopkins the year he portrayed the villain Hannibal Lector. Speaking of taking on this bizarre and unlikely assignment, he said the part came easily to him once he could hear the character's voice. My work as a secondary translator is a lot like that: once I've heard the lyrical voice of the text, choices of phrasing and vocabulary and shaping the work become nearly automatic, giving the poem a chance to have its character sustained and its energies passed on from one line to the next.

RICK LONDON

Original text: Ibrahim Nasrallah, *Sahara*, *Khiyam*, and *Sa'reer* from *Maraya Al-Ghobar*. Jordan: Al-shorouk, 1991.

صحـارى

.. في التراب صحارى
هي الحزنُ حينَ تهبُّ المنافي
حيثُ يحتارُ نهرٌ بأعشابهِ
حينَ ينسى ضفافي
وتَستَعِرُ الحربُ في ضحكاتِ النهارِ الأخيرِ
وينسى أليفي وعوديَ للبحرِ في صدره
وزهورَ اعترافي
في التراب صحارى تحنُّ إليّ
لتنسى اخضراري
ونعناعَ ظلّي على العتباتِ
وتذكرني –حينما يُذكَرُ الراحلونَ بعيداً–
بحُمَّى جفافي

Deserts

There are deserts in the dust causing heartache in exile.
A river becomes confused by its grasses
and forgets me and war blazes in the laughter of the last day.
My soul's other forgets the promises I made to the sea
and the flowers of my confessions.
In the dust there are deserts longing to forget my greenness
and the mint of my shadow on the doorsteps.
They only remember me—when those who've gone far away
are remembered—
by the dryness of my fever.

خيـــــام

في الترابِ خيامٌ
من الدّم .. والذعرِ
مُشرَعةٌ لفضاء الأساطيرِ في دَمِنا
وخيامٌ من الريحِ
تَحمِلُنا ..
للمكان الجديد ونحنُ هنا
حولَنا بعضُ رائحةِ البحرِ
شيءٌ من الكِلس في (الميجنا)
ها تكاثرَ فينا المُغني ..
تكاثرَ فينا الإمامُ
تكاثرَ فينا المذيعُ
تكاثرَ فينا الكلامُ
تكاثرَ فينا الرحيلُ
الوسامُ ..
وفتَّتَ بالنصر أجسادَنا!!
ولما نـزل بعدَ خمسينَ عاماً
– كما ذاتِ قَتْلٍ –
هنا.. وحدَنا

A Bed

In the dust there's a bed of whiteness
from which to look upon
our relatives' prayers,
and a flute,
supplications,
flowers of bitterness,
a silence that foretells startled trees in darkness,
and a wasteland reserved for graves
so that the stones are not wasted.
In the dust there's a bed of yearning for our roots
and our losses.
There's a universe that will arise
in the morning—made graceful by the living—
to conceal its violence in the dust.

سريـــر

في الترابِ سريرُ البياضِ الْمُطِلِّ
على صلواتِ الأقاربِ والنايِ
والدّعواتِ
وزهرِ المرارةْ
وصمتٍ يؤدي إلى شجرٍ خائفٍ في الظلامِ
وقَفْرٍ يَشيدُ القبورَ
لكيْ
لا تضيعَ الحجارَة !!
في الترابِ سريرُ الحنينِ إلى أصلِنا والخسارَةْ
وكونٌ سينهُضُ عندَ الصباحِ
– رشيقاً بأحيائه –
كي يُخبِئَ تحتَ الترابِ دمارَهْ

Tents

There are tents of blood and terror
in the dust
pitched there to make a myth of the sky.
There are tents of wind in our blood
that take us everywhere though we appear motionless,
so the lime in the lore of the *mejana*
and a smell from the sea surround us.
The singer has multiplied in us.
The Imam has multiplied in us.
The broadcaster has multiplied in us.
Talk has multiplied in us.
Departure and the medallions of war multiply and
fragment our bodies with victory!
And we are still here,
fifty years old—steeped in killing—
and on our own.

Thirteen Harbors

Suong Nguyet Minh | Translated by Charles Waugh and Nguyen Lien from Vietnamese (Vietnam)

The issue of helping those suffering from exposure to Agent Orange has become a cultural focal point in Vietnam, where a day rarely goes by without mention of some performance, art exhibit, television program, or benefit appearing in the national media. In many ways, this attention can be regarded as a consequence of literature's role as a social and political motivating force.

In the early 1990s, a journalist named Minh Chuyen began a series of essays on veterans and their families affected by Agent Orange. Birth defects, mental disorders, crippling contractures of the hands and feet, blindness, skin disorders, diabetes, and a variety of cancers have all been linked to exposure to dioxin, the toxic byproduct present at abnormally high levels in the chemical defoliants used by the U.S. military in Vietnam from 1961 to 1971. Chuyen's essays helped Vietnamese society begin to understand how some of the poorest people in the most remote areas were suffering the worst, to recognize that these illnesses were not simply a matter of fate to be borne by individuals alone, and to make clear the need for assistance.

Since then, a support group, the Vietnamese Association of the Victims of Agent Orange, has filed a lawsuit in an American court against the manufacturers of the defoliants. The suit was dismissed in 2005 and is currently being appealed. But all the while, Vietnamese writers have continued to work with this theme, in a remarkably diverse variety of ways, amplifying their readers' compassion.

This story, "Thirteen Harbors," by Suong Nguyet Minh, blends a traditional Vietnamese folk tale with the fate of a woman married to an exposed veteran. The author is a veteran himself, and now the fiction editor for the Army's *Literature and Art Magazine*. He has published three collections of short stories and has garnered several of Vietnam's most prestigious literary prizes.

I first worked with Nguyen Lien at Vietnam National University in 2005, where we planned the anthology this story is taken from. Lien provided the first draft, conveying the gist of each sentence's meaning. I followed by going back to the original Vietnamese and, wherever possible, restoring the initial syntax, metaphors, and idiomatic language. We were also able to work with Minh, discussing various problems to ensure that the best possible sense of the story would be conveyed.

CHARLES WAUGH

Original text: Suong Nguyet Minh, *Mười ba bến nước*.
Hanoi: Youth Publishing House, 2005.

Mười ba bến nước

Tôi lấy vợ mới cho chồng.

Một chuyện lạ chưa từng xảy ra ở làng Yên Hạ. Cô dâu là bạn thân của tôi đã quá lứa lỡ thì. Cô ấy đang cần tấm chồng và khao khát một đứa con hợp pháp. Tôi làm bà mối, tôi cùng nhà trai đi ăn hỏi, đi xin cưới, đi rước dâu.

Đám cưới có vui, có buồn, có sượng sùng. Và đúng lúc cô dâu mới vào buồng hạnh phúc thì tôi lặng lẽ ra lối cửa sau đi tắt qua vườn. Túi đồ ôm vào lòng, vừa đi vừa khóc, tôi chạy cùn cụt ra bến nước, ới đò sang sông về nhà với mẹ.

Người ta ví: Con gái mười hai bến nước. Tôi khốn nạn hơn những người đàn bà khác. Tôi những mười ba bến nước.

II

Tôi sinh nở lần đầu vào một buổi trưa.

Tháng năm âm lịch, cuối vụ gặt, tôi đem cơm ra đồng cho thợ. Cào cào, muỗm muỗm dồn đến đám lúa cuối cùng nhiều quá. Thợ gặt bỏ liềm hái vồ tới tấp. Tôi cũng đạp gốc rạ lội sọp sọp đến chộp. Tự nhiên, bụng đau lâm râm, rồi cồn lên đau dữ dội. Tôi vội bỏ nắm cào cào đã vặt càng vào nón và ôm bụng. Chưa kịp lên bờ thì ối vỡ, nước ối chảy ướt sũng hai ống quần. Tôi ới chồng. Anh bỏ đon lúa đang bó dở, hốt hoảng chạy đến bế tôi lên bờ. Mẹ chồng tôi quýnh quáng sai đứa cháu gọi bà đỡ đẻ. Nhưng không kịp, tôi đẻ ngay trên bờ ruộng ẩm ướt ngổn ngang lúa tươi và cuống rạ vừa cắt.

"Ối giời cao... đất dày ơi...ời!" Mẹ chồng tôi gào lên và xỉu ngay bên đon lúa. Tôi chỉ kịp cố gồng...

Thirteen Harbors

I took a new wife for my husband.

Maybe the strangest thing ever to happen at Yen Ha village, the bride was my good friend, a woman who had passed the age for marriage but for a long time had desired a child, and wanted a husband. Besides making the match, I helped my husband's sister and mother during the engagement ceremony and wedding, preparing dishes for their celebration.

Of course, for the others, the wedding had its share of happiness, but for me it held only humiliation and sorrow. Just at the moment when my husband took his new bride to the bedroom, I slipped silently through the back door and into the garden. Bag in hand, I wept while walking the road down to the river. I called for a ferry and crossed back to my mother's home.

There is a saying, *A girl has twelve harbors*, meaning only at the last will she find shelter. It took me thirteen.

II

I had gone into labor the first time at noon.

It was the fifth lunar month and the harvest was nearly finished. I had brought rice and corn and sweet potatoes to the harvesters in the field. Grasshoppers swarmed over the paddy, their wings clacking and sputtering. The harvesters had to throw down their sickles and chase after them. Kicking through the stubble, I waded into the paddy too. Suddenly I had a pain in my belly that very rapidly became worse and worse. I threw my grasshoppers into my hat and held my belly. My water broke, soaking my trousers before I reached the field's edge. I called to my husband. Bewildered, he dropped the unfinished sheaf of rice plants from his hands, ran over and lowered me in his arms to the ground. My mother-in-law nearly lost her head sending our nephew for a midwife. But it was too late. I gave birth right there on the wet earth, surrounded by the new rice plants on one side and the stubble of the old on the other.

"There's so much . . . the earth is soaked . . . oh!" cried my mother-in-law.

Terrified by my mother-in-law's mournful cry, I raised my head to look at my belly, and nearly fainted when I saw what I had given birth to: instead of a baby, just a piece of bloody, red meat. It had a dark mouth which looked like a fish running aground and yawning before dying. The mud-spattered harvesters gathered round, splashing and tramping in from all over the field.

"Put it in a pot and bury it in the Serpent Mound," said someone.

"No, put it on a banana tree raft and float it down the river," said another.

After this, I didn't leave the house and cried all the time, my silent husband looking after me as carefully as a little child. Tears brimmed in my mother-in-law's eyes when she looked at my emaciated face. She treated me like her own daughter.

One day, I asked her sadly, "Mother, how have I come to this?"

She breathed a sigh and said, "All the members of our family are kind-hearted people. We did not sow the breeze that resulted in this whirlwind on your body."

Just then, my husband accidentally dropped a pot of medicine. The pot broke and the wet yellow medicine plopped all over the floor, its steam rising.

I lost sleep frequently. Sometimes in my dreams I saw the harvesters wearing conical hats, sitting on the lawn and smoking tobacco while waiting for that piece of meat to stop yawning. After a while they put it in a terracotta pot. Then they took it to the Serpent Mound and buried it. Sometimes I had another dream in which they put my piece of red meat on a banana tree raft and floated it down the Hoang Long. Then a serpent monster with long black hair would surface from the depths and push the raft back to the riverbank. After either of these dreams I would wake with a start, yelling, "Give back my baby! Give me my baby!"

Opening my eyes, I'd find my husband holding me in his arms, my body cold with sweat. He held me this way through many nightmares.

III

During the summer of the year of the rooster, there was little rain in our village, but the water roared in from upstream for a whole week, catching my village in a heavy flood. The river flowed full of big logs and branches. The dike broke at midnight, releasing a thunderous swell. Dogs howled, and the chickens clucked madly, inciting the cows and buffaloes and goats to bawl and break down the gates of their stables. Panicky villagers ran here and there seeking safety. Just as I climbed to the top of a banyan tree, the river swallowed the village. I sat in the tree for hours, calling in the dim moonlight for my mother, terrified the serpent monster would come and drown me. Under the pull of the water, the banyan first began to lean, then uprooted and washed away. Hungry and exhausted, I was swept away by the flood.

I awoke the next morning to find myself sprawled on the Serpent Mound. Many villagers had gathered there, some standing, some sitting on their heels. The floodwaters moiled all around us.

A dog barked. My mother-in-law looked at me sadly, surprising me when she said: "It was the serpent monster that saved you and brought you to the mound."

At sixteen, I had met a team of archaeology students who came to my village to excavate the Serpent Mound. I knew one of the students, a boy named Tao, who had also grown up in Yen Ha village. He seemed to sympathize with me and liked to tease me. They excavated all week without finding anything but the shells of mussels and shipworms, animal bones and a wooden plank. Before replacing the dirt, Tao threw a straw doll into the pit.

"It's magic to use against any girl who might love and then betray me," he said. "It will turn the traitor into a serpent monster."

All the students laughed while I blushed with shame and confusion. Later, when we fell in love with each other, I asked him about the straw doll, but he wouldn't answer except with an enigmatic smile.

Despite the students' failure to turn anything up, stories about the mound persisted. One had it that during a moonlit night, a dense mist covered the river. The waves popped and echoed from a cave carved by the river in a limestone karst. A thief returning home in the dark could not find a ferry, so he began to remove his clothes, intending to carry them across on his head with the things he had stolen. Just then, a fishing boat glided silently to the riverbank. A boatgirl whose ragged shirt exposed her breast sat at the rudder.

"Come aboard," she said. "I'll take you across."

The thief climbed into the boat and, thinking indecent thoughts, happily found no one else aboard. When they reached the middle of the river, he advanced on the girl. Without hesitation, she slipped over the edge of the boat into the water, where he saw that only the upper part of her body appeared to be human. The lower half tapered into the long, wriggling tail of a serpent. Horror welled up inside him as he realized he had just embraced a serpent monster. Dumbfounded, he watched the head, bare shoulders and breasts of the girl emerge from the water. With both hands on the bow, she tipped the boat to let the water rush in, sinking it immediately. The thief could have drowned, but fortunately the current pushed him to shore instead. Trembling, he scrambled up the bank, but the serpent monster called him back: "Don't go! You forgot your bag."

When he turned, he found the girl as he first saw her. Her dry trouser cuffs had been rolled up around her thighs, revealing pale, human legs. She stood in the boat at the river's edge, holding the bag out to him, its many stolen things and the bag itself all completely dry. She let the bag drop to shore, then rowed into the mist and disappeared. After that night, obsessed with those events, the thief suffered from bouts of madness for half a year.

But to me, half a year is nothing: all my young life has been haunted by the serpent monster and the misty harbor.

IV

My husband's name was Lang. As a soldier bound for the front, he received a few weeks of leave before going to war. At first he didn't want to get married. Instead, he spent most of his time wandering around the village visiting relatives and friends, laughing and joking and drinking as if he would not return. When the leave was nearly finished, under great pressure from his mother, he hastened to find a woman who would agree to marry him. I met him while still grieving for Tao, who I'd heard had died at the front.

As a bride I was taken to my husband's house by boat. While the wedding party went ashore, I dipped water into a large gourd jar. According to village custom, this water would be used to wash the feet of my husband's mother. I don't know when the custom became popular in these villages, but people say it helps to prevent the fatal rivalry between mothers- and daughters-in-law, and I think they might be right. Before the wedding, my mother gave me the dry gourd jar along with instructions for acting and working as a good daughter-in-law.

Of course at that time, I knew the saying, *A girl has twelve harbors*, but I didn't yet know how many I would have to pass.

The wedding procession climbed slowly up the hill to where a large crowd had gathered and was shouting angrily. Suddenly I recognized Tao, my former lover, in the middle with a whitewashed flat basket hung around his neck that said, *I am a deserter.* I couldn't believe the man burdened with that flat basket was my lover. When all the areas in the north had been overwhelmed by American bombing, most schools had closed, and Tao joined the army. It had been reported that he had died in a battle on the front line. But now, the rumor running through the crowd had him so afraid of battle that he shot himself in the foot. Court-martialled, he had been sent home to be reeducated, which now appeared to mean being paraded around the village by a group of militiamen who condemned him as a deserter and traitor to his country. Tao limped ahead, followed by the militiamen carrying their AK-47s on their shoulders, urging him to call out: "I am a coward! I betrayed my country!"

Many kids followed them, jeering and repeating in unison: "I am a coward! I betrayed my country!"

Walking by the side of my husband, feeling such a pang in my heart, I did not know what to say.

One day after the wedding, Lang left for the front. We had no idea how long it would be before we met each other again. He tried to hide his sorrow, rushing through his farewells and leaving the village quickly.

V

During the war, a woman suffered terribly living without her husband. Many endless and sleepless nights I lay on the bed, longing for a kiss or an embrace. Heartbroken, I would cover my face with his old shirt. I suffered much more just before my time of the month, when my breasts would swell with a slight pain and my cheeks turn pink, my eyes glittering with desire.

During those long nights, many things happened in my imagination. When I smelled his shirt, it seemed I could smell the faint odor of his breath as well. But this only worked for a short while. To distract myself, I had to put paddy into the grinder and husk rice all night long. Sometimes I went to the well and ceaselessly poured buckets of cold water over my body, and sometimes I would go to my mother-in-law's bed and lie by her side because her breath was similar to my husband's.

Since my mother-in-law had her own experience of the days waiting for her husband from the front, she knew how I felt and thought she could help me. She put Lang's underwear in a pan and simmered them over a low flame, stirring them with a stick while murmuring her prayers. She believed this ritual helped a daughter-in-law be faithful to a husband far away.

Yen Ha village had two places along the riverside where villagers usually came to bathe: one upstream for women, the other, some two hundred meters downstream, for men. The women usually waded into the river without taking off their clothes. Away from the bank where the water rose high to their chests, they would roll their shirts to their heads like turbans and swim and wash themselves.

One of my many troubles came from bathing at this

river. On a hot day while walking with his men along the riverside, the chief of the militia discovered Tao and me swimming together. The chief bitterly hated draft dodgers and deserters. It galled him to believe these cowards seemed to have the time and opportunity to flirt with the wives of the soldiers fighting on the front lines. Of course he felt so strongly about it because his own wife had been caught having an affair with a ferry-boat worker and later became pregnant. As a result, he often spied on the women who talked with the workers at the riverside.

"I had a cramp," I insisted to the chief. "This man saved me from drowning."

Frightened, Tao stammered, "I heard her… cry for help when I… when I brought my… buffalo cart… to the river."

The militiamen wanted to take me and Tao to the Commune Administration, where they would interrogate us about our relationship. Tao wore only pants and walked lamely behind me. My black silk trousers clung wetly to my skin. I hadn't had time to put on my blouse, so I had just a camisole on my upper body. Suddenly, the chief told me to stop and put on my blouse. He changed his mind about the interrogation and sent me home.

"I'm letting you go," he said, "not because you deserve it, but out of consideration for the man at the front."

Nevertheless, as I walked away, I heard him cursing me behind my back, complaining about "faithless women."

VI

When the war ended, my husband came home. Seeing him return whole and unharmed loosed a flood of happiness, both in me as well as the rest of the family. But Lang became peevish just a few days later. The incident at the river had made me notorious in the village, and I had no idea how to explain my relationship with Tao to him. One evening, a host of friends and relatives came to our house, celebrating Lang's return as merrily as if it were Tet. But after they left, a funeral gloom settled on our home.

Sensing the cause of his mood, my mother-in-law

said to Lang, "I'm sorry for not having been able to keep a good reputation for your wife."

"I survived the war for many years," said Lang, "only to have this bad reputation kill me now."

Coldly, I said, "I am your wife. Only you can know whether I've been faithful or not."

Embarrassed and surprised, Lang mulled over what I had said. He could not decide whether to make our marriage work or to divorce me. As a soldier who had been far away from home for such a long time, it was difficult for him to know his own heart.

One night shortly thereafter, during a windy and very cool full moon, no one in the village could sleep. Nearly everyone gathered outside to enjoy the moonlight sparkling between the fishing boats anchored on the Hoang Long. But Lang and I stayed inside, lying on the bed and listening to the continuous clatter echoing back from the river where the fishermen knocked oars against their hulls to attract fish. When Lang's hand accidentally brushed against my body, I took it in my own. With this one touch, everything changed and we embraced each other passionately.

My mother-in-law got up early the next morning. She sat on the verandah, combing her hair and looking toward our bedroom now and then. When Lang stepped from our room, he sat by her side.

"Luckily, I kept my patience these past few days," he said. "If not, I might have murdered that bastard deserter, Tao, and ruined my marriage."

"What do you mean?" asked his mother.

"The one night after my marriage before I left for the war was Sao's time of the month," said Lang. "We just held each other and wept."

"Do you mean your wife is still a virgin?"

"Yes, until last night."

My mother-in-law was embarrassed and sat quietly. I stepped from the bedroom and rolled my hair with my hands. When gazing at myself in the mirror, I found my eyes bright and flowing with happiness. Then I sat by her side with a light heart.

"I didn't believe the rumor about you," she said. "But we had no witness to restore your reputation until now. Forgive me and don't be angry with me for what I've allowed to happen to you."

I laid my hand on her arm. "I am not angry with anyone. And I've never been afraid of anything, except that the war would prevent my husband from coming home. Only he could truly know how I've longed for his return."

VII

I gave birth to pieces of red meat at the end of my second, third and fourth pregnancies. Frightened and sad, my mother-in-law spent most of her time praying to the Buddha. But Buddha never came to help us. People say, *A wife's one hundred joys are not her husband's debts*, but all the members of my husband's family were virtuous, and yet I still had to bear this burden. Where did it come from?

I would not have thought it possible, but my womb produced even greater terrors during my fifth pregnancy. Several round balls of red meat emerged this time, like the red, leathery eggs a serpent monster might lay. But neither human nor devil would hatch from what I had carried for so many months and with so much pain.

Some villagers began to despise and shun me. One day, a pack of kids followed me, shouting, "Crazy woman! Crazy woman!"

Later my husband told me about the things I couldn't remember doing. I lost many hours wandering along the side of the Hoang Long river, slipping into the water, taking wild flowers and scattering them on the shore. Apparently I did this many times. Once I went to the Serpent Mound, where many small memorials had been raised for all the village's dead children. But I didn't know which ones belonged to my pieces of red meat.

VIII

One night the river ran low, and my husband and I went shrimping. Boat lamps sparkled all over the water, and the shrimp eyes reflecting the light became innumerable red dots glittering just beneath the surface. Once we had cast the net on the river, Lang pitched a tent for us on the Serpent Mound. If there were very few shrimp or fish to catch, we would sleep in the tent until morning. But this night, after catching half a basket of shrimp, I became tired and went to the tent to rest. Some time in the night I heard a woman call: "Give back my baby!"

A woman stepped down from the top of the mound, shouting: "They drowned my baby at the river. Help me! Give back my baby!"

"Are you crazy?" I told her. "You don't have a baby, you never…"

"Yes, I do," she interrupted. "That's my baby! Don't drown my baby, please."

I looked to where she pointed on the river and saw Tao putting pieces of red meat on a banana tree raft. The woman jumped down from the riverbank into the water. Then a serpent with a girl's upper body and long black hair rose to the surface and pushed the raft to shore. My heart filled with terror and I looked around, but Tao

and the raft had disappeared. Only a flock of wild white ducks flew low over the river, quacking.

"Sao! Sao!" Lang clapped my shoulders. "Are you okay?"

"It was Mrs. Sao who called for help," I said, still not fully conscious. "It was Mrs. Sao who jumped down to the river and turned into the serpent."

"Are you out of your mind? *You* are Sao, my wife." His eyes searched my own. "Let's go to the river, let's cast the net."

And so we cast the net until dawn.

On the way to the market to sell the shrimp, I met Tao, who carried terracotta pots in his buffalo cart.

"I hate those pots, Tao," I said. "They look terrible. Stop carrying them in your cart."

"Okay, but why do you hate them so much?"

I told him about my nightmare and said, "Do you remember when you came with the students to excavate the Serpent Mound, and you buried a straw doll in the pit? Why did you do that?"

Tao laughed. "It made no sense. I was just teasing.

But the straw doll legend is real, from the war between Vietnam and the Cham, who lived here many centuries ago. Under the reign of Tran Nghe Tong, the Cham navy came up the Hoang Long river from the sea, killing many people and burning the villages along the river. But strangely, they did nothing to Yen Ha village. When Tran Khat Chan, the Vietnamese general, defeated Che Bong Nga, the Cham general, the invaders fled to the sea. Only our village survived the war intact. But three months later, a lot of things became known more terrible than the fate of the villages destroyed by war. Scores of unmarried girls in our village turned out to be pregnant.

"The elders shaved the girls' heads and marked them with lime, then tied the girls to banana tree rafts and floated them down the river. But although the rafts floated downstream in the morning, by evening they had been pushed back to the village by hundreds of shrimp, fish, serpents and turtles. The elders became angry and directed the young men in the village to push the rafts downstream, but again and again they came back. Finally, the villagers gave up and freed the poor girls from their punishment. Many months later these girls gave birth to curly-haired, dark-skinned and wild-eyed children who didn't have the same flesh and blood as the villagers.

"Among those women, one gave birth to a piece of red meat with a round mouth that looked like a copper penny. Immediately, the villagers took the piece of red meat for a devil and floated it down the river. The young woman went mad, screaming incessantly: 'Give back my baby! Give me my baby!' At night, she went to the Hoang Long to look for her child. She waded into the river, swimming and diving all over, but could not find her baby. At last, exhausted, she slipped under the water and drowned. Then by some magic her body transformed into a serpent and washed ashore. The villagers buried the serpent body with copper pennies, tortoise shells and a girl-shaped straw doll on an island in the middle of the river. They even built a tomb for her. That's how this place became the Serpent Mound. They hoped honoring her would help to prevent such a terrible thing from happening again. The legend says the woman's soul still wanders the river and caves it passes. When a person might drown in the river, the woman changes into a serpent and saves her life.

"To pray for that woman's soul, you should put a clod of earth on the mound. Have you?"

"No, we didn't know."

"That's too bad. You should do it now."

IX

My husband and I walked the twelve kilometers into town to receive medical exams at the provincial hospital. The doctor told us: "Both of you are in good health and none of your test results explain Mrs. Sao's abnormal childbirths. We'd like you to visit a hospital in Hanoi, if you can you get there."

Lang told me to sell a cow at the market. His mother gave us a pair of earrings. Lang's younger sister gave us two breeding pigs, and my mother gave us a hundred kilos of paddy. We sold it all, except the earrings, which we planned to use to pay for medicine. "Nothing is more important than life," we thought. "If we have our health, we can make more money."

We went to the hospital in Hanoi and had at least ten different kinds of tests. The doctor finally said he could find nothing wrong with me, but he wanted to have a private talk with Lang, and asked me to leave the room.

Afterward, Lang told me the doctor said the dioxin level in his blood was very high. He took him to a laboratory to see hundreds of glass jars containing various kinds of deformed fetuses. The doctor explained: "In some cases, soldiers affected by Agent Orange can still give birth to normal children, but who knows what will happen when their children have children, or when all this will end?"

After returning home, Lang lay quietly on the bed for three days. His face sagged with exhaustion, making him look much older than his age.

"My darling," he said finally, "I don't want to lie to you. The doctor thinks I've been affected by Agent

Orange. He thinks if we keep trying to have children, we'll probably keep having these deformities."

"Agent Orange?" I exclaimed. "You must have known!"

"How could I know?" said Lang. "I feel fine. But after speaking with the doctor, I thought about the defoliated forests we had to cross. We drank water from streams running through them and even put some in our canteens. Once, in the jungle, we watched American planes flying slowly overhead spraying a dense white mist. A few days later, the leaves shriveled and came down easily in the breeze. All the trees withered and turned the color of death."

Wrapped in my husband's heart, I felt a pain there like one I'd not yet seen. Withered and bitter myself, I had no comfort to pour into him.

x

Lang received a letter from Ha Van Nenh, a former comrade, announcing that his new wife had just given birth to a son. Lang asked me to prepare some gifts for a visit to Nenh's family: a dozen eggs and several kilos of sticky rice.

Nenh's family lived in a stilt house built on a green hill in the mountains. When we arrived, the door was open, and the sound of a baby crying came from inside. A little girl, with no arms and no hair on her red head, stood by the stilts baring her teeth in a grin like a monkey. Afraid to be bitten, I hid behind my husband.

Surprised and pleased to see us, Nenh welcomed us to his home. Nenh's wife, Thuy, carried her baby in her arms and gave us a cheery hello.

"Your wife looks young and healthy," I told Nenh, and asked her to let me hold the baby.

"My first wife had three pregnancies," said Nenh, "but each produced deformities like you see with this one here. After her birth, my wife was so tired and frightened she abandoned us. Thuy is my new wife."

Suddenly during the conversation, Lang's face turned white. "Where did you get these water barrels?" he asked.

Nenh said after the war, he had been assigned to a

project building a veterans' cemetery. He and his friends had found many barrels scattered in the forest that they thought might be used for water. One of Nenh's comrades was a lorry driver, and helped transport the barrels to their villages in the North.

"My god! What stupidity!" cried Lang. "You've brought death to your family. These defoliant containers are what deformed your children."

Nenh's face wrinkled and turned pale.

XI

After returning home from Nenh's, Lang told his mother about Nenh's marrying a new wife who gave birth to a healthy son. After thinking it over for several days, Lang explained his decision for making a change in our lives: "A new marriage might bring us better luck. Who knows?"

Lang said he hoped if I married a healthy man, I might have normal children and a good family. Upset by Lang's proposal, I kept silent for many days.

One day, when Lang was out, my mother-in-law came to my bedroom and asked, "What do you think for the future of your little family?"

"I have no idea," I said. I still didn't want to talk. But she was patient with me, despite my disrespectful tone.

"I am not so selfish as to think only of Lang," said my mother-in-law. "I have always treated you as my own daughter. I wish some change would be good for both of you."

"So you want me to leave my husband and allow him to marry a new wife," I said, crying. "But can you be sure his new wife will give birth to a healthy child?"

"No one could be sure of anything in such a situation," she said, "but let's try." Suddenly she knelt down to me. "My darling, I beg you to show mercy to Lang, to our family and to yourself. You might have a better life with a healthy husband."

"Oh, Mother!" I said, taking her hands in mine. "I am grateful for your kindness and good will, but let me think carefully before I tell you what I feel we must do."

Sadly, I found myself clinging to the hope for a

normal life and child and agreed with my mother-in-law to try again, repeating in my mind what Lang had said: "Who knows?"

XII

After helping my husband marry a new wife, I went back to my own mother's home, where she took pity on me, weeping. Half a year passed. I couldn't forget the days and nights when Lang and I worked hard for our living, the smell of sweat from his shirt and face, the long days when I expected good or bad news of him from the front, or the long nights when we slept in the tent by the river and cast our nets for shrimp. Of course, neither could I forget my five terrible births.

I often went to the riverside at sunset and looked at my former husband's house, where the cook smoke rose from the thatch roof into the sky. Did he remember me when he slept with his new wife?

I knew the cause of my misfortune after visiting the hospital with Lang, but the straw doll Tao buried in the Serpent Mound still haunted me. One day I took a pick and shovel and crossed the river to the Serpent Mound. I dug for hours.

I had just begun to drag out a skeleton when Tao drifted by in his boat.

"Tao," I cried, "This is the serpent monster that destroyed my life."

"That's crazy," said Tao. "That story was just a joke."

"This isn't a skeleton of a serpent monster?"

"It's just some animal."

"Why did you lie to me? That serpent monster story has haunted me for so long."

"Forget the serpent monster," he said. "You have something more important to worry about."

I looked at him expectantly.

"Stay calm, okay? Lang's new wife has just given birth to eleven pieces of red meat."

I began to tremble.

"Sao, my darling…"

A ringing sounded in my ears. "Lang and me," I murmured, "it's hard to tell who's more miserable."

XIII

I had to cross the river again.

My friend could not bear the burden of my husband's house. After the miscarriage, she left quickly. Lang clenched his teeth and endured the disaster, even while his mother had become seriously ill. They needed my help more than ever, leaving me no choice but to try my thirteenth harbor.

I chose to cross at night. A dense mist covered the river, the ferry barely visible from the flickering of the boatgirl's cookfire. Once on board, I noticed the many terracotta pots inside the boat, and my limbs went limp with fear. When we reached the middle of the river, dozens of banana tree rafts began to bump into us, blocking our way. The boatgirl used her pole to repel the rafts. But after one raft had been pushed away, another came back again, swarming with the others all around. "We can't get through here," cried the boatgirl. "We have to turn back and cross somewhere else."

"This is the last harbor," I insisted. "We must cross here."

I helped the girl push the rafts away. Finally they dispersed, and the ferry crossed the river, my hardest crossing yet.

Once ashore, I turned to the river and found the banana tree rafts had vanished. The boat and the boatgirl sank into the mist, and the last thing I saw was the terracotta pots under the boat's dim light fading away.

Focus on Turkish Poetry

Contemporary Turkish poetry, as represented by this handful of vivid and powerful voices, is vibrant, mysterious, alluringly textured, and more than a little wild at times, often residing just at the edge of the rational, everyday world. Indeed, in his introduction to his recent anthology, *Eda: An Anthology of Contemporary Turkish Poetry,* editor Murat Nemet-Nejat insists that the essence of the Turkish language itself resides in its fundamental structure that insists on the mysterious, hidden relations of things. According to Nemet-Nejat, "the underlying syntactical principle is not logic, but emphasis: a movement of the speaker's or writer's affections." The language, being agglutinative, requires a fair dose of patience and intuition, as often one never knows the true intention of the speaker until one gets to the end of a very long sentence. The poems here, whose subjects are made of such disparate issues as masks, sex, fortune-telling, the disintegration of culture, and, of course, love, each make use of the resonance of intention, a vivid and distinct cultural heritage, and, everywhere, that most poetic and mysterious of tropes, metaphor. I hope, if this is your first encounter with Turkish poetry, that you will be delighted and intrigued enough to look more deeply into this exciting literature at this vivid moment in its history.

SIDNEY WADE

Two Poems by Murathan Mungan

Translated by Aron Aji from Turkish (Turkey)

Murathan Mungan has authored over fifty literary works, including twenty books of poetry, and he enjoys possibly the most diverse readership in Turkey. He is certainly not a conventional bestseller, given his steady focus on the politics of gender, sexual orientation, ethnicity and religion—topics that continue to provoke uneasy divisions among the Turkish public. Politics and culture are deeply personal for Mungan; his characters invariably inhabit difficult landscapes of depersonalizing norms, taboos, hierarchies and ideologies, as they struggle for authenticity.

Mungan's attention to the rich particularity of human stories translates into an irresistible lyricism in his poetry. Most of his poems feature the lover addressing a beloved, and draw from two complementary currents. The first is the romance tradition, including the likes of *Laila and Majnun*, and *Ferhad and Shirin*, which lends universality to Mungan's treatment of love. The second is the private reserve of memories of the particular love affair that occasions a given poem. While the first current renders the poems familiar and elicits pathos, the second presents what ultimately remains enigmatic and inaccessible about love, the private core wherein the experience liberates the actors. Especially since the love invoked in these poems is most commonly homoerotic, the interplay of these currents results in contesting the prevailing notions of eros/romance, and affirming the taboo as a locus of self-authentication.

Concerning the translation process, two dimensions of Mungan's poetry deserve particular mention. First is his juxtaposition of "stock" romantic imagery and diction with private and enigmatic ones. Consider, for instance, the use of the stock epithet, "my love" and desert imagery (common to several traditional romances) inside what is essentially a catalogue of inaccessibly personal yet obviously intentional and precise references: "The leopards are dead, my love, so are the tigers, the jaguars / the desertless bedouins are the new subjects of the plains." The second dimension involves Mungan's lineation and syntax, specifically his idiosyncratic punctuation, his inversion of conventional syntax combined with "linked couplets," in which a line can semantically complement both the preceding and superseding lines (i.e., lines 23–29 in "The Snow Prince"). Together, these two features give Mungan's reader (and translator) a sense of freedom and participation in the making of meaning; paradoxically, they also render all interpretation (outside that of the poet) unstable and contingent.

Original text: Murathan Mungan, "Kar Prensi" from *Başkalarının Gecesi*. Istanbul: Metis, 1997. "Maske" from *Metal*. Istanbul: Metis, 1994.

Kar Prensi

Karlı fundalıklarda bırak, kalın uykuların sabahında
yaşamın saf değerlerini
çekil başkalarının aynalarından
omuzlarında ödünç pelerin
ceplerinde kurşun paralar
bütün bunlar sana göre değil
Eldivenlerini çıkar, kırağı uçuğu çiçeklere
denizmercanlarına, sefer ateşleri yakmış
balıkçı teknelerine bak
sonra kayatuzu, şeytankınası,
ucu ağulu kargılarla kendine başla
bak şimdiden
deliller ve ayrıntılarla kan tutuyor geceyi

eşik altına saklanan bir anahtar
kuyuların ıslak bilezikleri

The Snow Prince

There, among the snow-covered heather
in the morning after the deep sleep
drop those pure virtues of life
walk away from other people's mirrors
a borrowed cape on your shoulders
lead coins in your pockets
all these are not for you
Remove your gloves
Look at the frost-singed flowers, the coral reefs
the fishing boats, their seafaring lanterns
then take the rock-salt, devil's henna
the poison-tipped reeds, and begin making yourself
look: already the night is stunned
by the evidence and the fine details

a key tucked under the door

düz, sakin, kendinle konuşur gibi dene
kanını yenileyen serüveni
kav gibi gizli ateş,
ten gibi lav
sorgusuz sevişsek
uykunun beyaz yasası teslim almadan bizi

ne duello kanunları, ne görünmez kelepçeler
tabiatı keşfeder
kutuplarından ekvatoruna
kendin indir doğal afetlerini
haritanı sağlamlaştır
anıların ve geleceğin için
iki kişi olana kadar yaz kendini
biri emekli bir hayalet
Shakespeare sonesi
öteki, mahzun şiirlerin yedek yolcusu
bir kar prensi

Döndüğünde orada olacağım
Karlı fundalıklarda bekleyeceğim seni

wet rings around the wells
try—calmly, plainly, as if talking to yourself—
the adventure that renews your blood
the avid secret fire
the skin-like lava
that if we made love unquestioning
before the white law of sleep overtakes us

codes of the duel or invisible hand-cuffs
neither will discover nature
from your poles to your equator
bring down your own natural disasters
authenticate your map
for your memories and your future
write yourself until there are two of you
one, retired ghost
a Shakespearean sonnet
the other, a standby traveler of doleful poems
a snow prince

When you return I will be there
among the snow-covered heather, waiting for you

Maske

Maske ölmek isteğidir sevgilim
gerisingeriye dönen etiket
bak gökyüzünde takma bulutlar
ümitlerini yükseğe ayarla
ve bataklık halılarında dinlen
ey kutsal beden
sana da gelecek sıra
pilindeki kuraklık yetmiyor değil mi
hatıranın yüksek gerilimine
başkalarının bantlarında batıp çıkıyor sesin
kağıttan intihar kuleleri
eteklerinde dipnotlarıyla devrildi tek tek
bilgisayarların depoladığı vahşetten çıkış alıyor
yeni bir maskenin formülleri
granite dönüşsün diye iskelet ve etiket
Doğru, kolay silinebilir bir muşambadır seks

Mask

The mask is a death-wish, my love
a label turning back on itself
look; false clouds in the sky
set your hopes up high
lean back on quicksand carpets
o sacred body
your turn too will come
your dried up battery cannot withstand, can it
the high voltage of memory
your voice rises and falls on other people's tapes
the paper suicide towers have tumbled one by one
with footnotes at their heels
violence stored in hard-drives engenders
the formulas for a new mask
to turn the skeleton and the label into granite
True, sex is an oilcloth, easy to wipe

ateşten geçirir karton filmleri
bazukalar altında kadife gece
leoparlar öldü sevgilim, parslar, jaguarlar
çölü olmayan bedeviler platoların yeni özneleri

yırtılan bir yara izi sevgilim baktığın aynalar
tinerle sil maskeni, ekrandaki görüntünü ayarla
volümünü kıs kalbinin, dahili hatta seni arıyorlar

a fire that singes cartoon films
a velvet night captive to bazookas
the leopards are dead, my love, so are the tigers, the jaguars
the desertless bedouins are the new subjects of the plains

a wound scar tearing open, my love, those mirrors you look in
wipe your mask with turpentine, adjust your image on the screen
lower your heart's volume, they are calling you on the intercom

Two Contemporary Turkish Women Poets

Gülten Akın and Zeynep Uzunbay | Translated from Turkish (Turkey) by the Cunda Translation Workshop

Gülten Akın (born in Yozgat in 1933) is one of Turkey's most honored and distinguished poets. After her graduation from Ankara University, she practiced law in several parts of Anatolia, accompanied by her husband, a government administrator. The mother of five children, she has lived for many years now in Ankara.

The poet began writing at eighteen, and her first collection *Rüzgar Saati* won a poetry prize in 1956. Since then she has published over fifteen books of poetry and several collections of essays. Now the *doyenne* of Turkish poetry with many awards, Gülten Akın continues to write, despite ill health. Her poetry, a quiet testimony to resilience against suffering and oppression, stands as the vibrant voice of a strong, individual, feminine social conscience.

Zeynep Uzunbay (born in Kayseri in 1961) belongs to the highly promising generation of younger Turkish poets. Before getting her degree in Turkish literature she worked as a nurse. Since 1995 she has published four collections of poetry: (*Sabahçı Su Kıyıları* / Morning Water Shores; *Yaşamaşk* / Lifelove, 1998; *Kim'e* / Who For, 2003; *Yara Falı* / Telling Wounds, 2006). She received awards for her poetry in 1998 and 2004.

Both poets were guests at the first Cunda International Workshop for Translators of Turkish Literature (CWTTL), held for two weeks in June 2006. Founded by Saliha Paker in 2005 and supported by the Turkish Ministry of Culture, the CWTTL hosts translators of Turkish literature from within Turkey and abroad. At special sessions of the workshop devoted to the guest speakers, Gülten Akın spoke in great detail about the relationship between her life and her work, while Zeynep Uzunbay provided background for her poem "With Your Voice" (from *Kim'e* / Who For). It arose, she said, from feelings associated with a special kind of coat that she and others of her class had to wear at a boarding school. In it the poet rebels against the forced conformity of appearance, a major issue now in Turkish politics.

As it happened, two versions of "Sesinle" were pro-

duced in addition to the one printed here. Ronald Tamplin and Saliha Paker's version, entitled "Voice," appeared in the spring 2007 issue of *Near East Review*, and Kurt Heinzelman produced a third version. "Done With the City" (from *Kuş Uçsa Gölge Kalır* / Bird Flies, Shadow Stays) was translated at the June 2007 session of the Cunda Workshop as part of a project initiated by the CWTTL to translate Gülten Akın's recent poetry. Arzu Eker and Cemal Demircioğlu selected a number of her poems and prepared drafts on which they worked with poet and translator Sidney Wade and myself.

MEL KENNE

Original texts: Gülten Akın, *Kuş Uçsa Gölge Kalır*. Istanbul: Yapı Kredi Yayınları, 2007. Zeynep Uzunbay, *Kim'e*. Istanbul: Papirüs Yayınevi, 2003.

Sesinle

mor imgeli deli pardösümün altında
çıplağım, usulca açıyor sesin düğmelerimi
önce o öpüyor omuzlarımdan

adın kapatıyor dudaklarımı
içime eriyor gitmek

mor imgeli deli pardösüm düşüyor yere
çırılçıplak sarılıyor belime sesin
koşuyor koşuyor yetişemiyoruz ırmağa

ZEYNEP UZUNBAY

With Your Voice

under my spring coat's zany purple pattern lies
my nakedness, gently your voice opens unbuttons me
from my shoulders first kissing me

shutting my lips with your name
a letting go melts into me

my spring coat of zany purple designs drops
with your voice stripped naked clutching my waist
on and on we run, still no match for the river

Translated by SALIHA PAKER
and MEL KENNE

Kent Bitti

Yakın sesler gitti
geceler el değiştirdi, yıkımlar
anılmıyor bile dilden çıktı
çözülme gündemde

antenlerin uyduların metalik söylemiyle
birleşilemiyor
yabancı isimler trafik imleri alarm zilleri
arasında karşılaşanlar
tanışıyorlar mı? tanışamıyorlar
bu bir çarpışmaya benziyor
bütün gün bütün gün çarpışa
kentin ağır sularında
herkes yaralı
erkekler

Done with the City

Voices closeby gone
nights have changed hands, demolitions
not even mentioned, left tongues
disintegration on the agenda

no one can unite
with the metallic discourse of antennas and satellites
do those who encounter each other
in the midst of foreign names traffic signs alarm bells
really meet? they can't
this is more like a collision
crashing crashing all day crashing
in the city's heavy waters
everyone wounded
men

kanına alkolden kıymıklar batıran
erkekler doğuyor çılgınlıklarından
kadınlarsa
kapatıp kendilerini rahimlerine
sırlarıyla oynuyorlar

kent bitti

GÜLTEN AKIN

pricking into their blood alcohol splinters
men being born out of their madness
women
shutting themselves up in their wombs
playing with their secrets

done
with the city

Translated by CEMAL DEMIRCIOĞLU,
ARZU EKER and MEL KENNE

Poems by Seyhan Erozçelik and Sami Baydar

Translated by Murat Nemet-Nejat from Turkish (Turkey)

In Seyhan Erozçelik's *Rosestrikes and Coffee Grinds* (*Gül ve Telve*), the Shamanistic/Islamic forces underlying the Turkish culture are in full view and dialectic tension. *Coffee Grinds* consists of twenty-four coffee grind readings of fortune, from the residues of grinds left in the cup and in the saucer after Turkish coffee is drunk. Here is how the process works:

"Water is time, the mysterious catalyst in the fate of coffee grinds. What determines the fate of an arrangement, its reading? The drinker of coffee, the cadence and strength of the lips, as they sip the coffee, how far to the drains, how much liquid is left in the cup. The drinker then turns down the cup (like cutting a deck of cards).

How long does the turned down cup lie fallow, the grinds trickling down along the sides of the cup. As water dries, the fortune sets; once set, they can only crumble.

Then the reader interprets the coffee grinds.

A coffee grind reading is a spirit echo of the world, consisting of the same four elements: earth, the coffee grinds; water, the liquid in which they move (time); wind, the voice of the reader; and fire, the urgent queries of the listener (also moon, his/her passion) which try to rush the dilatory rhythm of fortune, its telling."

Fortune telling is an old Shamanistic tradition from Central Asia. The great achievement of Erozçelik's *Coffee Grinds* is to bring the animistic/pantheistic impulse of this tradition into the twenty-first century. In this view animal spirits of nature and cosmological forces are in a constant process of change and interaction and in the almost chaotic magic of these metamorphoses one sees reflections of human hope, desire, and longing.

The task of the translator of *Coffee Grinds* is to evoke the dilatory rhythms of the teller, the seductive, teasing, humorous interchange he/she establishes with the listener of the fortune, pulling both the listener and the reader of the poem into its magical, soulful, yearning universe.

Though dealing with a few of the same Sufi symbols, "the rose" and "the nightingale," Sami Baydar's poetry, including "Poem of Dust" ("Toz Siiri") from his book *Çiçek Dünyalar* (Flowers of the World), published in 1996, focuses on the chaotic dimension of the Sufi

equation. This poetry is about the soul's dissolution, the spirit of water in Sufism, a kind of negative ecstasy which explores the limits of reason, barely pointing to the order which may lie beyond. Sami Baydar's poetry and his language stand at a point of suspended disintegration of consciousness (*The Arc of Descent*) just at the moment before they may turn around towards a new union.

The biggest challenge in translating Sami Baydar is not to "improve" on the poems, trying to bring some order or reason or form to them; but to let its peculiar light, the daring extremeness of his linguistic abandon, what the Turkish poet Lale Müldür calls the light "under the leaf," shine through.

Original Text: Seyhan Erozçelik's *Gül ve Telve* is forthcoming from Talisman House in 2008. Sami Baydar, "Toz Siiri" from *Çiçek Dünyalar*. Istanbul: Yapi Kredi Yayınları, 1996.

Telve

Üç

Maske takıp, karışıyorsun kalabalığa. Hayvanlarla insanların bir arada oldukları bir kalabalık. Kanatlı bir cüce, yahut cüce bir melek, seyrediyor her şeyi.

Ellerinde balıklar ve kuşlar var. Atıyor kalabalığın üzerine. Kuşlar uçuyor, balıklar insanların gözlerine dalıyor ve yüzmeye başlıyor. Solungaçlar, insanların irislerini yırtıyor. Uçan kuşlar, ateş topları kusuyor.

Kuşlar kötü. Balıklar kötü. Kanatlı cüce, yahut cüce melek, o da kötü.

Sakın kendini, maskeyi takma, kalabalığa karışma! (*O, italik*, kalabalığa karışma…)

Kalabalıktaki insanlar, ruhlarını karıştırıp kukla oynatıyorlar gökte.

Aydınlık bir mesafeden, rüzgâr gibi biri geliyor. (Rüzgârgibi gelmiyor. Yani *zarf* değil. Kendisi rüzgâr gibi. Duruşu, bakışı, her şeyiyle…)

Coffee Grinds

Three

Wearing a mask, you're mingling with a crowd. There, beasts and human beings together…
A midget with wings, or a midget angel, is viewing everything…

Holding fish and birds. Casts them over the crowd. Birds are flying. Fish diving into people's
eyes, trying to swim. The fins are tearing folks' irises. The flying birds are regurgitating
balls of fire.

Birds are bad news, fish, bad news, the winged midget, bad news, the midget angel, also
bad news…

Don't *you* ever, donning your mask, lose yourself in the crowd. (These folks are *all* leaning
sideways, in *italics*. Don't ever mix with them…)

People, exchanging souls, are pulling each others' strings, in the sky.

Dağıtıyor kalabalığı, kuşları, balıkları, ateş toplarını, kanatlı cüceyi, yahut cüce meleği…

Senin kalbinde de, iyi yürekli bir horoz ortaya çıkıyor, doğuyor içine…

Masal gibi bir fal işte!

From a lit up distance a man like the wind is approaching. (He is not coming like the wind, that is, *adverbially*, he's the wind, standing straight, looking every way…)

He's dispersing the clouds, the birds, the fish, the balls of fire, the winged midget, or the midget angel…

And in your heart, also, a good hearted rooster is rising, is being born…

This fortune reads *exactly* like a fairy tale. *Exactly.*

Yirmi

(Falını bir türlü kapatamadın. Bunun adı, fal telaşı.)

Fal fincanın dışına taştı.

Dışarıdan başlıyorum.

Dışarıda, yani fincanın dışında, falın içine kaçmaya çalışan, ya da fala girmeye çalışan bir hayvan var. Küçük, yırtıcı, tüyleri güzel, kuyruğu uzun. Önündeki yol da açık.

O küçük, yırtıcı hayvan, falın içine suretini göndermiş. Telveden bir suret, içeride salınıp duruyor. Elini kolunu sallaya sallaya, kendi yurdunda dolaşıyormuş gibi.

Yüzü olmayan biri, bayrak taşıyor. (Falında yine bayrak çıktı.)

Orman hayvanları, hep birlikte şarkı söylüyorlar.

Twenty

(You 'ere unable to settle your fortune. This is called coffee grind anxiety.)

The grinds have overflown the cup.

I'll start outside.

In other words outside the cup, there is an animal trying to escape inside, or trying to *enter* your fortune. Small, ferocious, beautiful hair… with a long tail. And the path before it wide open.

That *small*, ferocious beast has sent its *replica* inside. A replica of coffee grinds oscillating inside, keeps strolling, swinging its arms, as if it owned the place, in its own country.

A person without a face, holding a flag. *(The flag's appeared in your cup again!)*

Forest beasts, singing all together.

İçinin kabarıklığı, zar gibi bir telve haline gelmiş, püf desen yırtılacak.

(Püf!)

Küçük, yırtıcı hayvanın suretinin sureti de, fincanın içinde.

Artık, fincanın içi ayrı bir dünya, ayrı bir âlem.

O âlem, büyüyor.

Tabaktan fincana bir ırmak akıyor. Telve ırmağı.

Fal hayvanı, hani şu yırtıcı hayvan, ırmakta boğuluyor.

Fincanda yeniden doğuyor.

Bir başka türlü söylersek, eşik atlıyor.

Başka bir âleme—

SEYHAN EROZCELIK

The swollen, bubbly places inside have stretched the coffee grinds like a membrane. If I say *piff!* It will burst.

(Piff!)

And the replica of the replica of the small beast also is in the cup.

Now inside the cup a universe apart, a separate world.

That world, expanding.

From the cup to the saucer a rivulet is running, a rivulet of grinds.

The beast of fortune, that very ferocious one, is drowning in this brook.

Reborn in the cup.

To put it in another way, it's jumped a threshold.

To another world…

Toz Şiiri

Toz bana geldi
beni işitmek için
kapladı
kısa sözcüklerle
bir felaket habercisi gibi.

İşitmek için bir bülbül eğildi
bir çiçeğin ağzından
bir söylence gibi.

Şimdi hangi yöne dönsem
söyleyemeyeceğim
bir yanlış
bir şiir
yaşamın yeni yeri.

The Poem of Dust

Dust came
to hear me
covered me
in short words
like an announcer of catastrophe.

To hear, a
nightingale stooped
from a flower's opening
like a gossip.

I can't guess
whichever way I turn now
if an error
a poem
the new locus of life.

En kaba sözler
kuşların içinde kemik
insanlar gelecek dedikleri gökte
gerçek leylekleri.

Belki bir yönden gelecekler yine
eskisi gibi bir dil
bulunsa
çözülebilecek belki şiirleri.

Gül çekirdekleri
bir gözde şimdi
karanlık kelimeleri yok ediyor
ağzında sessizlik dedikleri dikeni.

SAMI BAYDAR

Vulgarest words
bones inside birds
cranes of truth
flowing in the sky people call the future.

Maybe from some direction they'll appear
as they used to
if a language is found
poems maybe solved.

Seeds of the rose
are in an eye now
darkness is making words vanish
in its opening the thorny stem called silence.

Contributors

A native of Turkey, **Aron Aji** has translated fiction by Murathan Mungan, Elif Shafak, and Latife Tekin, as well as two book-length works by Bilge Karasu: *Death in Troy* (City Lights, 2002) and *The Garden of Departed Cats* (New Directions, 2004), which received ALTA's 2004 National Translation Award. He is also the recipient of a 2006 NEA Literature Fellowship for his current translation project, a third novel by Karasu, *The Evening of a Very Long Day*. Aji is a professor at St. Ambrose University-Davenport, Iowa.

Omnia Amin was born in Cairo, Egypt. She graduated from the American University in Cairo and received an MA and PhD in modern and contemporary British literature from the University of London, Queen Mary and Westfield College. Former chair of the English department at Philadelphia University in Jordan, Amin currently teaches at Zayed University in UAE.

Chris Andrews teaches at the University of Melbourne. In 2005 he received the Valle-Inclán Prize for his translation of Roberto Bolaño's *Distant Star*, and the PEN Translation Fund Award for Bolaño's *Last Evenings on Earth*. His translations of other Spanish-language writers include César Aira and Carmen Posadas.

Trudy Balch's translations include *Gaby Brimmer*, by Gaby Brimmer and Elena Poniatowska (forthcoming from the University Press of New England), subtitles for the Ladino dialogue in the film *Novia que te vea*, and numerous essays on Spanish and Latin American art, photography, and culture.

Douglas Basford's translations appear, or are forthcoming, in *Poetry, Subtropics,* and *Smartish Pace,* and he has poems and prose in *32 Poems, The Texas Review, Slant, The National Poetry Review,* and elsewhere. He teaches at Johns Hopkins, edits the online journal unsplendid.com, and has a chapbook due out next year.

Josephine Berganza is a translator and short-story writer. She was born and spent her childhood in Britain, then moved to France, where she lived first in Grenoble, then in Brittany, before her studies in literature and linguistics brought her to California.

Wendy Burk is the translator of Tedi López Mills' *While Light Is Built.* Her poems and translations have appeared in various journals, and have been anthologized in *Connecting Lines: New Poetry from Mexico,* from Sarabande Books, and the Kore Press audio anthology *Autumnal: A Collection of Elegies.*

Artist, writer, and translator, **Inara Cedrins** has a BA in writing from Columbia College and an MA in arts administration from the School of the Art Institute of Chicago. Her anthology of contemporary Latvian poetry was published by the University of Iowa Press, and she is currently working on a new Baltic anthology.

Jessica Cohen was born in England, raised in Israel, and now lives in the U.S.A. She translates contemporary Israeli prose and poetry, as well as commercial material from and into Hebrew. Her published translations include David Grossman's award-winning *Her Body Knows,* and critically acclaimed works by Yael Hedaya, Ronit Matalon, Amir Gutfreund, and Tom Segev.

Margaret Jull Costa has translated more than sixty books by Spanish and Portuguese writers, amongst them

Bernardo Atxaga, Fernando Pessoa, and José Saramago. She has won various translation prizes, the most recent of which was the 2006 Premio Valle-Inclán for *Your Face Tomorrow: Fever and Spear* by Javier Marías.

Sean Cotter worked in Romania as a Peace Corps volunteer and Fulbright scholar. His Romanian translations include *Second-Hand Souls: Selected Writings of Nichita Danilov* and *Goldsmith Market* by Liliana Ursu. Cotter has been published in *Hayden's Ferry Review* and *Conjunctions*, among others. He teaches literature and translation studies at the University of Texas, Dallas.

Cemal Demircioğlu is Assistant Professor of translation studies at Okan University, Istanbul, Turkey. He completed his BA and MA in Turkish language and iterature and PhD in translation studies at Bogaziçi University. He is the member of the Cunda International Workshop for Translators of Turkish Literature (CWTTL).

Arzu Eker teaches English and translation courses at Bogaziçi University, where she is currently working on her PhD thesis on Orhan Pamuk's translations into English.

John Estes is a doctoral student and instructor at the University of Missouri in Columbia. Recent poems have appeared or are forthcoming in *Circumference, Zoland Poetry, Ninth Letter, The Journal, Notre Dame Review*, and *Literary Imagination*. His chapbook, *Breakfast with Blake at the Laocoön*, is available from Finishing Line Press.

Ken Fontenot holds an MA in German from the University of Texas at Austin. His translations from German, as well as his own poems, have been published widely. His two books of poetry are *After the Days of Miami* and *All My Animals and Stars*.

Edward Gauvin translates children's graphic novels for First Second Books and three ongoing comics series for

Archaia Studios Press. His work on fabulist Georges-Olivier Châteaureynaud, the author's first appearance in English, may be seen at *AGNI*'s online magazine and among other pieces at Words Without Borders.

Margret Grebowicz's translations have appeared in numerous journals, including *Agni, Poetry International, World Literature Today,* and *Field.* She teaches philosophy at Goucher College and publishes in the areas of gender studies, science studies, and post-structuralism. Her most recent work may be found in *Hypatia: A Journal of Feminist Philosophy* and the edited collection *SciFi in the Mind's Eye: Reading Science through Science Fiction.* She is currently at work on two book-length projects: a monograph about Jean-François Lyotard and feminist theory, and a volume of translations of Ewa Lipska's poetry.

Acclaimed for her best-selling translation of Cervantes' *Don Quixote*, and an anthology of Spanish Renaissance poetry entitled *The Golden Age*, **Edith Grossman** is best known for her translations of modern Latin American authors, including Gabriel García Márquez, Mario Vargas Llosa, Carlos Fuentes, Álvaro Mutis, and Mayra Montero. Grossman is the recipient of the 2006 PEN Ralph Manheim Award for Translation, and her recent translations of Vargas Llosa's *The Bad Girl* (Farrar, Straus & Giroux) and Montero's *Dancing to "Almendra"* (Farrar, Straus & Giroux) were both included in *The New York Times Book Review*'s "100 Notable Books of 2007."

Marilyn Hacker's books of poems include *Essays on Departure* (Carcanet, 2006) and *Desesperanto* (Norton, 2003). Recent translations include Vénus Khoury-Ghata's *Nettles* (Graywolf, 2008) and Guy Goffette's *Charlestown Blues* (University of Chicago, 2007). She received the first Robert Fagles Translation Prize for Marie Etienne's *King of a Hundred Horsemen*, to be published by Farrar, Straus & Giroux.

Michael Henry Heim teaches Russian and Central European literature at UCLA. His translations from

Russian, Czech, Serbo-Croatian, Hungarian, German, and French include works by Anton Chekhov, Milan Kundera, Bohumil Hrabal, Günter Grass, and Thomas Mann.

Devadatta Joardar's co-translation, with Joe Winter, of Nobel Prize-winning poet Rabindranath Tagore's *Of Myself* was released in 2006 by Anvil Press in England and Visva-Bharati in India. Joardar lives in Kolkata and writes regularly for English-language dailies in India.

Mel Kenne teaches literature at Kadir Has University in Istanbul. He has written four books of poetry and translated many poems from Spanish and Turkish into English. With Saliha Paker he translated Latife Tekin's novels *Dear Shameless Death* (*Sevgili Arsız Ölüm*) and *Swords of Ice* (*Buzdan Kılıclar*), both Marion Boyars Publications.

Alexis Levitin's translations have appeared in *Partisan Review*, *Grand Street*, and *American Poetry Review*.

He recently translated Eugénio de Andrade's *Forbidden Words* and Carlos de Oliveira's *Guernica and Other Poems*. He was awarded residencies at the Banff International Center for Literary Translation and the European Translator's Collegium, and received an NEA Translation Fellowship.

Nguyen Lien is professor emeritus of American Literature at Vietnam National University, where he has taught for nearly fifty years. He runs a publishing house in Hanoi, and, with Charles Waugh, recently received a Rockefeller grant to collect and translate literature about Agent Orange exposure during the Vietnam War.

Rick London's most recent publication is the chapbook *Picture With Moving Parts* (Doorjamb Press, 2002). He lives and works in San Francisco.

Elizabeth Gamble Miller, PhD, is professor emerita at Southern Methodist University, serves on the board of *Translation Review*, and is a corresponding member of the Academia Salvadoreña de la Lengua. Miller has published translations by more than thirty authors, and has lectured and led literary translation workshops in six nations.

Murat Nemet-Nejat edited *Eda: An Anthology of Contemporary Turkish Poetry* (Talisman House, 2004). His translations, poems, and essays include Ece Ayhan's *A Blind Cat Black* and *Orthodoxies*, Orhan Veli's *I, Orhan Veli*, and *The Peripheral Space of Photography*. He is presently translating Seyhan Erozçelik's *Rosestrikes and Coffee Grinds* (*Gül ve Telve*).

Elizabeth Novickas is a graduate of the University of Illinois, with a BA in rhetoric from the Urbana campus and a MA in Lithuanian language and literature from the Chicago campus. She has worked previously as a bookbinder, newspaper designer, cartographer, and computer system administrator.

Saliha Paker is a professor of translation studies at Bogaziçi University in Istanbul. Various essays and translations of hers have appeared in international publications, and she has co-translated three novels by Latife Tekin. She recently edited and co-translated the selection of Enis Batur's poetry *Ash Divan* (Talisman House).

Jordan Mills Pleasant is a member of the American Literary Translators Association. His translations have appeared in the *Journal of Italian Translation* and *Gradiva Magazine*, and in 2004 he was awarded the Poetry Prize from the Northern Kentucky Writers' Alliance for his original poems. Pleasant is currently studying classical Arabic at the American University in Cairo.

Ivy Porpotage is a technical editor working on an MFA in creative writing at American University, where she also teaches college writing. Outside of literary translation, she focuses on writing creative non-fiction and fiction. She also spends much of her time trying to broker peace between her two persnickety cats and two jocund dogs at her home in Arlington, Virginia.

José Edmundo Ocampo Reyes was born and raised in the Philippines and holds an MFA from Columbia University. His translations of Filipino poems have appeared or are forthcoming in *Circumference, Ploughshares*, and *Poetry International*; and his own poems have appeared or are forthcoming in *American Literary Review, Hudson Review, Michigan Quarterly Review*, and *Pleiades*.

Lawrence Venuti translates from Italian, French, and Catalan. Recent translations include Antonia Pozzi's *Breath: Poems and Letters* (2002), the anthology *Italy:*

A Traveler's Literary Companion (2003), and Massimo Carlotto's crime novel *The Goodbye Kiss* (2006). He is the author of *The Translator's Invisibility* (2nd ed., 2008).

Charles Waugh's stories and essays have appeared in *Sycamore Review, B/N Magazine, Wisconsin Review, Knock, Proteus*, and *ISLE*. He teaches at Utah State University and is the fiction editor of *Isotope*. The story "Thirteen Harbors" is from a collection for whose translation he and Nguyen Lien received a 2006 Rockefeller Foundation Fellowship.

Editors

Prose editor **John Biguenet** is the author of *The Torturer's Apprentice: Stories* and the novel *Oyster*. His play *Rising Water* won the National New Plays Network Commission Award for 2006 and was nominated for the Pulitzer Prize. An O. Henry award winner and *New York Times* guest columnist, Biguenet was twice elected president of the American Literary Translators Association and has published two volumes on literary translation. He is the Robert Hunter Distinguished Professor at Loyola University in New Orleans.

Poetry editor **Sidney Wade** is a recent president of the Associated Writers and Writing Programs (AWP) and is currently a professor at the University of Florida in Gainesville, where she teaches poetry and translation workshops. Wade is the author of five collections of poetry: *Stroke*, *Celestial Bodies*, *Empty Sleeves*, *Green*, and *Istanbul'dan/From Istanbul*, which was published in Turkish and in English by Yapi kredi Yayinlari, Istanbul.

Index

by author

Index

by title

Index

by language

A Note on the Translations

Original texts appear across from their translations. Where feasible, the entire original text is provided for each of the translations; however, space concerns have prevented the inclusion of more than the first page of prose pieces. Excerpts are marked by spaced ellipses. Copyright permission remains the responsibility of the contributors.

In order to express regional differences in language usage, we make every attempt to locate the authors within the literary tradition of a particular country or geographical region. The region is indicated in parentheses following the language on each title page.

In selections by British translators, British spellings and language use are retained. However, punctuation may be changed to conform to TWO LINES styles.

All translations in this edition of TWO LINES are published in North America for the first time.

Acknowledgments

Sincere thanks to Maria Gould,
Amy Lin, Yara Badday,
and Noelle de la Paz for their work
on this book.

About TWO LINES

For fifteen years, TWO LINES has published translations of poetry and fiction from more than fifty languages and fifty countries. Every edition features the best in international writing, showcasing diverse new writing alongside the world's most celebrated literature and presenting exclusive insight from translators into the creative art of translation. Through the annual volume of TWO LINES World Writing in Translation and the World Library, TWO LINES opens the borders of world literature to give readers access to the most vibrant writing from around the world.

TWO LINES is a program of the Center for the Art of Translation, a non-profit organization that promotes international literature and translation through the arts, education, and community outreach. The Center aims to make global voices and great literature accessible to readers and communities through the TWO LINES publications; the Poetry Inside Out educational program, and Lit&Lunch, the only bilingual reading series spotlighting translation. The Center was created to bring readers and writers together across borders and languages. Through each of its programs, the Center promotes translation and world writing as a vital bridge not just between languages, but between people.

Order copies of TWO LINES or find out more about the Center at www.catranslation.org.

Ceist na Teangan

Nuala Ní Dhomhnaill

Cuirim mo dhóchas ar snámh
i mbáidín teangan
faoi mar a leagfá naíonán
i gcliabhán
a bheadh fite fuaite
de dhuilleoga feileastraim
is bitiúman agus pic
bheith cuimilte lena thóin

ansan é a leagadh síos
i measc na ngiolcach
is coigeal na mban sí
le taobh na habhann,
féachaint n'fheadaraís
cá dtabharfaidh an sruth é,
féachaint, dála Mhaoise,
an bhfóirfidh iníon Fhorainn?

The Language Issue

Translated by Ivy Porpotage from Gaelic

I set my hope afloat
in a little ark of language,
as you might set an infant
in a basket woven
of iris leaves,
strengthened
by bitumen and pitch.
Tenderly, lowering it

among the bulrushes
and sedge
at the edge of a river,
watching—not knowing
where the current might take it;
perhaps, like Moses,
to land at the feet
of a Pharaoh's daughter?